His grip tight[...] on her arms

He pulled her close, bent his head, brought his mouth down upon hers, seeking, demanding, and getting response. Suddenly she felt she was overdoing the response. Luenda tried to draw back.

He said indignantly, "What are you trying to do now? Look, we've had very few moments without misunderstanding till now, or few even alone. Don't you think this is nice?"

"Well, yes. I mean perhaps. But I think we were getting just a bit carried away by suddenly declaring a truce. Gwillym, I want to talk."

"This is much more enjoyable than talking." His tone was audacious. "Okay, and while you're talking I'll just undo that great thick jacket. I can't get anywhere near you with that on."

Luenda was conscious of that feeling of one's bones turning to water. She ought to resist that feeling; how could she be sure of this man? But...but it *was* nice.

Books by Essie Summers

HARLEQUIN ROMANCES

These books may be available at your local bookseller.

For a free catalog listing all titles currently available,
send your name and address to:

Harlequin Reader Service
2504 West Southern Avenue, Tempe, AZ 85282
Canadian address: Stratford, Ontario N5A 6W2

A Mountain for Luenda

Essie Summers

Harlequin Books

TORONTO • NEW YORK • LONDON
AMSTERDAM • PARIS • SYDNEY • HAMBURG
STOCKHOLM • ATHENS • TOKYO • MILAN

Original hardcover edition published in 1983
by Mills & Boon Limited

ISBN 0-373-02590-4

Harlequin Romance first edition December 1983

Dedicated to Luenda Scott, whose name I loved, and
whose husband, Duncan, shares with Bill and myself a
love of the high-country sheep stations.

CHAPTER ONE

LUENDA MORGAN woke to the serene beauty of an early autumn morning in Auckland, but as the recollection of besetting problems rushed in on her, she thought bitterly that the serenity of her surroundings was a mockery . . . everything, the glimpse of the bay from the window, the sun glinting on the white hulls of the moored craft, the symmetrical outline of Rangitoto floating like an oval jewel on the sparkling harbour, only served to remind her that they could stay here no longer.

Most of all she resented it for Judith and Diana, the twelve-year-old twins, and for Davy, two years younger. Till this last blow had fallen Luenda had felt herself able to cushion the shocks. They had recovered from the loss of their lovely, gay mother because life had gone on for them much as usual, with Luenda there, and their father, Tony Sherborne, Luenda's stepfather.

Then a certain rot had set in. They hadn't guessed how much Tony had depended upon his lighthearted wife. That gaiety of exterior had hidden a sturdiness of spirit that Tony had leaned upon. His doctor had advised a trip overseas . . . new scenes, new faces. It had seemed to work, at first. His desire to travel till he could face life without his Nicola had been understandable, but to borrow and borrow against all his assets was hard to forgive, especially when, finally, Luenda had realised most of it had gone at the gaming tables.

It had seemed to her like something out of another world, completely alien to theirs. Something read about that happened to other people, not to you. It was almost impossible to believe of that loved father-figure who had come into Luenda's life when she was eleven. Someone who had meant comfort, fun, security and love.

The trip she had made to Las Vegas, numbed and disbelieving, where he had suffered a massive coronary at the gaming table, still seemed like a remembered nightmare to her, though at the time she had attended to all the formalities with a sort of icy and efficient calm.

She had awakened from that frozen state only when, on return, the full extent of her stepfather's liabilities had been revealed. He had raised money against everything . . . his business, his insurances, even—and this was the worst blow of all—against their home.

They couldn't stay in it. It must be sold. The children had to know their circumstances were much changed, but in some way she had managed to keep from them the knowledge of their father's real, almost criminal, folly. They hadn't questioned the statement that without Dad earning, finance was much less plentiful than before.

She had got them through the long summer holidays of the New Zealand Christmas and settled back into their schools at the beginning of February by selling the family car, then the small one her mother had owned and which Luenda had found so handy for conveying the children to their various sports meetings and other social interests. The launch had gone too, and had fetched a big price, but money just melted.

Luenda turned her head away from the view. She would rather stare at the opposite wall. When the mortgages were repaid there wouldn't be enough to pay the necessary deposit on a smaller house in a less fashionable suburb, much less face the high interest rates of today's world, and the price of flats was prohibitive too. Her salary just wouldn't stretch that far. That knowledge had driven Luenda to near-panic in private, a week ago. Then had come that astounding yet shattering letter from a firm of Auckland solicitors, telling of the communication they had had from Californian counterparts, and from another in Queenstown in the Far South of the South Island here. And the proposition contained in that had brought just as many problems and difficult decisions with it.

Knowing that Megan Richards had died in California had saddened Luenda ... so new a friend had come into her life, yet in the short time she had been in Auckland last year, she had proved a kindred spirit despite the difference in their ages.

They were so short on relations, Megan had seemed like a breath from the past, bringing alive again the grandparents she had known and loved as a little girl, her own father's parents.

At first Megan had been just a pleasant voice on the phone saying she would like to come to see Luenda before she departed to spend a few months with a sister in California, but was spending a month in Auckland looking up old school friends. She had been a comfort to Luenda, sympathetic but not censorious that Tony Sherborne had left his children in Luenda's care while he travelled.

'Grief takes us in differing ways,' she had said. 'I hardly knew myself the first year after Evan died. Suddenly he'll get a yen for home, and head back.'

She had talked a lot about Luenda's grandparents, but only in the last day or two had she told Luenda how much, all unknowingly, she had owed them. 'They were rather older than I was, married, with one child— your father. Then I married and went off to the bottom of nowhere, as my family termed it. But how I loved it! A sheep station across a lake, with never a road to link it up. A kingdom all our own. And like you, as children, we'd lived on the water. Handling boats was second nature to me. I had a young sister up here.

'Then war broke out, and times weren't easy for anyone. Gillian was in love with a young fellow in camp. Their parents felt they were too young to marry, and I expect they were. Their feelings got the better of them on his final leave. He never even reached the Middle East—he died on the voyage. Gillian found out she was going to have his baby. Our parents kept it from me—they thought I was too far away to be upset. Communication was poor then, and we got our mail only once a fortnight.

'Your grandparents adopted the baby. Later on Gillian married an American serviceman. She lives in California now.'

Luenda had interrupted her. 'Not—Aunt Beverley? Oh, yes, it must be. I knew she was adopted, but nothing about it. I did wonder why she hadn't got a Welsh name. I loved my Aunt Beverley so much. But she's lived in Canada for so long now. We keep in touch by letters.'

Megan Richards had nodded. 'Your grandparents said Gillian must name her own baby. She'd always wanted a little girl called Beverley. It was like a miracle to Gillian, seemingly, when she went to Canada. They see quite a lot of each other. Gillian wrote me the whole story a few months ago when she knew I was coming to Auckland. She'd heard through Beverley of your mother's death and because it seemed like the last link with your grandparents, asked me if I'd come to see you. She's never forgotten what she owes to your family.' Megan sighed. 'Had I known, at the time, I'd have adopted the baby myself, but they thought then that I'd have a family of my own. We didn't. And in any case, it was so remote Gillian would hardly have seen her. It was better the way it happened.'

Megan had written to Luenda two or three times from California, and was looking forward to seeing her on return. She had hoped she might get office leave during some school holiday and bring the children to the sheep-station, but before Luenda had replied to that, the shock of her stepfather's death, and the circumstances, had shattered their lives.

Just when things seemed blackest had come the request for an appointment, from the Auckland solicitors. At first Mr Freemont had raised Luenda's hopes. He had said that in the information he had had from California and from Queenstown, Mrs Richards had felt much in debt to Luenda's family and would like to repay a great kindness done her, by Luenda's grandparents.

Luenda's heart had given a great bound of hope. It

would be a legacy ... she need have no qualms about taking it. It would be a godsend. It might make all the difference to her need for somewhere to live ... to an adequate deposit on modest quarters ... oh, if only it was!

Then suddenly she was listening to a most extraordinary proposition. If she went to live for a full year, with the children, at that remote sheep-station at the far side of Lake Moana-Kotare ... a sheep-station where still no roads ran ... where the only access was by launch from Ludwigtown, then their keep and half the income from the estate would be theirs for that twelve months. But—but how preposterous! If at the end of that time she decided to stay there, other arrangements not specified but very favourable, would be made for her.

Mr Freemont was most understanding. He let her regain her breath. Even then she could formulate no answer. He said quietly, 'This is nothing that can be decided quickly. You must have a week, at least, to think it over. It's a strange condition. Was she very eccentric?'

Luenda had to be honest. 'Not really. In fact, she was very sweet.' She said despairingly, 'If only it was a sheep-station in the Auckland province, I'd give it a go. Or—or anywhere in New Zealand less remote. I mean an area with a road running to its door, served by a school bus. And why—why should she want me to live there? And ... and who does live there?'

'There's a bit of detail available. The manager does. And quite a staff, there are two or three houses on the estate. It doesn't say if he's a relation or not, but he could be. Perhaps a nephew of the husband's. It's a Welsh name, Gwillym Lloyd Vaughan.'

Luenda nodded. 'They don't come any more Welsh than that. So it could be a relation.'

'It seems as soon as her sudden death occurred at her sister's, he flew there. They had a cremation service and her ashes are to be interred in the private burial-ground at the estate. He's as astounded as you are. He rang me from there, as a matter of fact. He sounds very down to earth—knows his own mind. He's going to call me and make an appointment when he flies in.' He cleared his throat. 'I think from what he said, he owns the other half of the property.'

Luenda blinked. 'What do you mean? I—I just get the income from half of it for this year, don't I? If I go.'

The solicitor said carefully, 'That's what it seems. Only what is to happen at the end of the twelvemonth is a matter of guesswork. I strongly advise you, in view of your present situation, which your late stepfather's man of business has acquainted me with, to accept this year there. It's a splendid chance for you, of marking time, and I should think, if Mrs. Richards has got you to move the family down there, and give up your job, there'll be something substantial for you at the end.'

Luenda still couldn't take it in. She bit her lip. 'I wish it were a little clearer. Won't her sister . . . Gillian . . . resent this? A year's income out of the estate to perfect strangers?'

Mr Freemont decided he liked this girl. Her stepfather's solicitor had spoken well of her. 'Not a perfect stranger as far as you're concerned, but the granddaughter of two people who came to her rescue when she most needed it, who gave her little daughter a happy home. Besides, something I've been told . . . Mrs Richards arranged long ago for her sister and her sister's children to share in a trust fund, in her lifetime. Everything that came to Mrs Richards from their parents was put into it, and a certain amount from the estate. And Gillian's husband owns supermarkets. Even so, they all get legacies now. So do the staff on the estate who've been there a long time. The housekeeper is to receive outright a house Mrs Richards owned in Ludwigtown, when she decides to retire.'

Luenda's voice wobbled. 'She might easily decide to retire when we—if we—descend upon her, a city girl with three children! In my opinion they're good youngsters, though high-spirited, but this could unsettle them. They've already come through a tough time. Of course,' a note of hope crept in, 'there may be other children there. Has this manager a family? Does he live in the main house? Or is there a manager's residence?'

She thought the solicitor's voice sounded rueful. 'He's a bachelor. Not particularly young, I'd think, though voices, on an international toll-line, are deceptive. I've suggested he call to meet you after he's seen us. He's coming through Auckland.'

'That's all it needed! A housekeeper nearing retiring age and a crusty old bachelor not used to children! He's probably a real curmudgeon. I ought to be thinking of this as a miracle ... the one I'd been praying for ... instead I'm faced with a situation that positively bristles with snags.' She looked up, caught the compassionate eye and said, 'I'm sorry, I'm being defeatist. It's just the children I'm worried about. Alone, I could take it. It's not so bad as if they were facing their School Certificate or University Entrance years, but I feel all gone at the knees when I think of how it could affect them, a major change like this in their life-style and educational system.'

Mr Freemont leaned forward, his hands clasped on his blotter. 'My dear, it could happen, even if at the end of this year you leave the Mount Serenity Station, that they'll look back on this year as the most marvellous experience of their lives.'

She looked doubtful. 'Might they?'

He said, smiling reminiscently, 'My life lies within this city now. But I was brought up in what we then called the backblocks, and in the middle of the Depression too. My parents owned a farm away up the Wanganui River ... accessible only by paddle-steamer. It was only by practising the most rigid economy that they managed to hang on it. When High School days came they had to give up the idea of boarding-school for their four sons and continue with correspondence lessons supervised by our mother. We made it. Later, as things improved, the two youngest even made it to university ... under our own steam, working in shearing gangs and right through all the vacations. One was myself, and my brother is a judge. Our two elder brothers are still on the property; they wanted no other life.

'We all feel we had the most wonderful childhood any children could have. Perhaps the war taught us that. With a housekeeper you'd be free to supervise the lessons,' he added. 'The homestead will be well equipped for it. There'll be a proper schoolroom. I've been in touch with my Queenstown colleague, and it's a well-run station. I'm sure, with a kindly-intentioned woman like this, that when it comes to the end of the year, she'll have left you some sort of security whatever you decide to do. I put it down as the whim of a childless woman, to see a girl she took a fancy to, and who came from a family who'd helped her young sister out, share in the prosperity of the estate.

'It's a splendid chance, once you've got over the shock of uprooting. The balance you'll have when mortgages are repaid won't be large, but it can be invested for the future, and for a year all your costs will be met. And who knows what provision Megan Richards will have made for you at the end of it? My dear . . . I respect the fact that all your concern is for the children, but they're more resilient than you think.'

Luenda felt the tears rush to her eyes at this kind tone. 'I consider myself fortunate in having you act for me in this. You've been very patient with me. I'll give it a go—I must.'

Her employer had been just as understanding, though rueful at losing the secretary he had found efficient and of whom he had grown very fond. She had been with him six years, from her raw junior days up. She wondered if she would ever get a position she liked as much if this whole thing proved a fiasco and unendurable.

She looked at her watch and sprang up. Thank goodness it would be a busy day . . . the autumn fashion parade at Ackroyd's. Not that it closely concerned Luenda, but Joseph Ackroyd would be like a cat on hot bricks all day and it would be full of minor crises hastily smoothed over so that the public would be unaware of spanners in the works.

The models would be elegantly calm outwardly, inwardly as temperamental as they come, and hers would be the task of keeping unforeseen interruptions away from Big Joe, bless him. He'd had so much strain himself the last few months, with the accident to his beloved daughter, but Tania had come through her ordeal superbly, despite the fact that she had been three months pregnant when it had happened to her.

Being so busy would keep private worries at bay. The children had taken it far better than Luenda had expected. If they loathed leaving their schools, their friends, their bay with its boats and beauty, they were hiding it well.

Diana's immediate reaction had been good and had set the trend for the others. Her great green eyes had lit up. 'A sheep-station? Luenda, any chance of a horse to ride?'

Luenda had recklessly assured her there would probably be dozens of horses. Judith's brown eyes had shown a similar sparkle, but her query had surprised her older sister. 'Will they have hens?'

Luenda burst out laughing. 'I'd no idea you had any fancy for poultry! Why——'

'Just that ever since I saw those battery hens all in their little coops, I've thought I'd like to own some in old-fashioned hen-houses like in that story-book I had when I was little. With big wire-netting runs.'

Luenda was cautious. 'Well, even some of the big farms have gone all production-minded, and might have batteries. So don't for heaven's sake start criticising as soon as you get there. Be tactful and they might let you have a hen and chickens of your own in time.'

Davy had set that uncompromisingly square chin of his and said, 'I won't budge unless Griff goes too.'

Luenda had known dismay. What if on a farm where dogs were working dogs and they were terrified of a pet dog becoming a sheep-worrier, they simply wouldn't allow them to take Griff? She'd played for time. 'We'll have to make sure it's okay about his injections and so on, Davy. If he can't come right away I'll put him in kennels till he can.'

Now Luenda showered, woke the children, put out their cereal, toasted bread, cut sandwiches for their lunches, and saw they had their homework books in their satchels. 'Judith, you're in charge of the pudding tonight. It's there, in that basin, already tied down. Switch that pan on at four-thirty and when it's boiling, put it in and make sure it doesn't go off the boil, and if the water boils away, add more from the kettle, but through that funnel so you don't scald yourself. The casserole only needs re-heating, so don't put it in till I get home because on parade day I might get held up. Di, you know what vegies. They can go on when I get home too. Get as much done of your homework as you can, then you'll be able to watch TV later. Davy, that goes for you too. I'm off. Have a good day!'

Her own day was much as she'd expected. The floral decorations for the mannequin parade arrived late, though they were glorious when they came. The designer discovered an infinitesimal speck of blood on the embroidery of the bridal gown, and threw a wobbly. An extra sequin was stitched on immediately. A child whose mother should have been looking after him better decided he'd try going *up* the *down* escalator and got thrown off, and the subsequent fuss by the mother took up half an hour of Luenda's time because everyone else was flat out.

Then Big Joe got word that Tania had started labour and was in the nursing home. In the afternoon the parade got under way and was well attended, and superbly done, from the first bar of music. Luenda was in attendance on Big Joe till it got well started then slipped away to catch up on her office duties. She found a note for her to ring Mr Freemont.

He said, 'I just wanted you to confirm that you can meet Mr Vaughan at one-fifteen on Friday.'

'Yes, my employer has kindly given me an extra hour on to my dinner-hour, so it will be fine. His plane gets in at six-forty a.m., you said, didn't you? So that should give him time to recover from his jet-lag ... possibly put him in a good humour. I certainly hope he's a good traveller.'

'Miss Morgan, don't get too worked up. Some bogeys are figments of our imaginations. This could be a kindly man and well used to his late employer's idiosyncrasies. He may even know more about it than we do.'

Her voice warmed. 'Oh, thank you! Though it would be natural for him to regard me as a cuckoo in the nest. But I can take it as long as he doesn't make the children feel unwanted. I'll be most happy if it turns out more harmoniously than I think.'

She had no time to worry more. Something much more frightening landed in her lap. Big Joe rushed in. 'Luenda ... along to the dressing-rooms! The most awful thing's happened. Zena's fallen off the dressing-stand and has either sprained her ankle or broken a small bone. They're taking her off to Casualty right now. You're the right height and about the same statistics and you walk beautifully. You know we've often had you trying on samples. Nobody will suspect you aren't a professional. Your colouring is excellent, even better than Zena's—hers is so blonde it's almost unnatural. But the streaky bits in yours would enhance it. There are only four dresses, all for evening. Come on, scram!'

She couldn't refuse, but at the very thought her mouth went dry, her knees wobbly. She clutched her boss's arm. 'How long have I got, Mr Ackroyd?'

'Half an hour. Time for superb make-up. Thank heaven those styles call for simple hair styles ... just with a deep swirl, and yours has it naturally ... a long pageboy ... and your fringe over to one side.'

She had a few moments of sheer terror at the unrehearsed ordeal ahead, then her heart steadied as Big Joe said, 'My son-in-law has just rung. Tania is *still* in the first stage. Say a prayer that everything goes all right, Luenda. She's gone through so much to land this baby safely on the shores of time.'

'I will, Mr Ackroyd. Now lead me on, and put up a prayer yourself that *I* don't fall off the platform!'

She was sure later that her adrenalin gland must have come to her aid, because all went without a hitch and she even enjoyed it . . . till she came to donning the last evening dress. She couldn't help giving a gasp of dismay and the dresser grinned. 'I know how you feel. Zena loves it, of course—she's that type. Try to get detached about it, love. We can't cut it out. It's in the catalogue . . . listed as the Kronenburg Sensation. And it *is* beautiful, if a little daring.'

'A *little*!' said Luenda, feelingly. 'Zena could carry it off, she's an exhibitionist. But me . . . oh dear! And I have a feeling there's slightly more of me to show . . . where it matters. Esther, the darned thing can't be worn with a bra, can it?' she gulped.

Esther said swiftly, 'You can't let Big Joe down. Not today. No temperament, please. On with it! And *think* yourself into the spirit of this dress. It's the peak of the parade.'

'I wish it had been the start of it,' said Luenda miserably. 'How can I carry this off? All right, I know it has to be done.'

Esther said, with an attempt at lightening the situation, 'And don't look like Mary Queen of Scots going to the block, either. You took part in that play the firm put on, as a last-minute stand-in, and did magnificently. Now, stand still.'

She stepped back, surveyed her handiwork, said, 'Do you know? Zena would turn green with jealousy to see you! The darker streaks in your hair are more effective with that pale flesh colour, and I prefer your brown eyes to Zena's green with it, too. The fact that this swathe of gauze will be across your shoulders for the entrance will break it down a bit for you.'

She made a practised swirl across Luenda's lovely shoulders with a length of the gauze that merged in shades from the muted flesh-pink to the deepest burgundy, and pinned it on the left with a silken rose whose heart was the deepest shade, the reverse of the

petals the palest ... a Kronenburg Rose. The first
glimpse was to be of a demure gown ... the dramatic
moment when the model was to unpin the rose, remove
the stole, give a sophisticated twirl, was to be in vivid,
provocative contrast.

A calmness descended upon Luenda. It had to be
done. She heard the compère's voice announcing her,
the soft music begin, dreamy, sensitive. Luenda went
forward through the pillars and glided down the walk.
She felt cool, detached, resigned. She entered into it
fully.

There was a gasp of admiration, then another, a
different one, as with studied nonchalance, then a quick
movement, she discarded the gauze. No one would have
known that she was saying to herself as she had done as
a little girl sweating it out in the dentist's chair, 'It'll be
over in a minute, a minute, a minute ...'

Just as she made her last pirouette and began to walk
back to the rose-wreathed pillars, she met the eyes of a
man standing a little apart from the seated groups. Till
now she had singled out no one from the sea of faces,
but it was the look on this man's face that momentarily
caught her attention. What could make anyone
interested in the world of fashion wear a look like that?
It was a compound of scorn, derision, almost of dislike.
How odd! He stood out curiously too in that gathering
of the élite of Auckland, plus interested rivals, well-
groomed business men.

They were in light summer suits. He was wearing an
open-necked short-sleeved sports shirt and very casual
trousers badly in need of a press. Luenda's glance
flicked on. What did a look like that matter? But she
had hated it.

It was wonderful to slide into one's own clothes
again, to feel the firmness of her lacy bra, to shrug into
her polka-dot blouse, white and brown, her trim brown
skirt. She received the praise and thanks of everyone,
and, very heartfelt, those of Big Joe himself.

They moved from the dressing-room into a small
staff-room, had a much-needed cup of tea and some

delightful refreshments sent across from the restaurant.

At last, happily, she was able to return to the dear and familiar surroundings of her own office. At last Mr Ackroyd joined her. He got cracking signing letters. He said worriedly, 'I don't think I dare ring that nursing home again to see if there's any progress. They think I'm worse than any expectant father already! They keep saying everything's going as well as can be expected . . . but then I don't know *what* they expect when a girl was tossed out of the door of a car and down a thirty-foot bank a third of the way through a pregnancy!'

Luenda said sturdily, 'They said at the time that if harm had been done to the baby, she'd have lost it then. I think a baby is well cushioned. And the last two months, Tania has been very well. This isn't a particularly long labour for a first.'

'Thanks, you're a great comfort.' They both jumped as the phone rang, which was stupid, considering it rang all day most of the time. Luenda answered, beamed, and handed it to her boss. 'Tania's husband.'

A few excited moments later Big Joe was saying to Luenda, 'A boy, eight and a half pounds and perfect. Tania's fine. I can get to see them in half an hour.'

He put out two great hands and hugged his secretary. She dropped a kiss on his chin lightly, than laughed. 'Some man just came to the office window, took one look, and turned hurriedly away. Oh, well, if it was one of the staff, he'll soon know it was sheer jubilation, not intrigue!'

Mr Ackroyd chuckled. 'You flatter me . . . at my age! I'll dash along and tell the heads of the departments. They are a great bunch, they've all been concerned. Order a celebration morning tea for them for tomorrow, will you?'

'They're concerned because you've been a great boss,' said Luenda, 'and your wife's a darling to them too. A great team, the whole family. Will you pick Mrs Ackroyd up on the way?'

'No, Bill said she was there. She'd gone to keep him company. Luenda, you've been a great scout today, in this emergency. And it's not an easy time for you just now. Take a taxi home tonight and charge it to the firm.'

Even though that made her earlier, it didn't mean they had dinner sooner than planned. The twins were full of what had happened. 'We've had a power cut, from the sub-station. A poor possum got in and up on the wires and must have swung round and its tail made contact with the other wire, I suppose ... we heard the bang from here!'

Luenda said, 'Davy's special pud will be ruined. It'd be off the boil for ages. We'll just open some tinned boysenberries.'

'No, the timing was good. Judith had just switched it on, and it wasn't boiling, so we waited till it came on again. We got the rest of the stuff ready.'

'Poor kids, I bet it seemed ages,' Luenda sympathised.

Di looked bland. 'No, not really. We used the time well.'

Luenda saw a warning look pass to her from Judith. 'I gather you didn't spend it doing homework?'

Judith replied quickly, 'Not entirely. But we've got a good start with that, just the same.'

Davy said scornfully, 'I could tell you what they were doing. Clunky things! They said they were going to have a family conference about our ... um ... our state of affairs and how they could help, and they wouldn't let me in on it. Stupid things ... I thought it could have been a really bright idea, but it was just dumb. Abso-bally-lutely dumb!'

Di pounced. '*You're* dumb. You're passing judgement on something you don't know about. We didn't let you in on it.'

Davy grinned evilly. 'That's what *you* think! I hid in the *pohutukawa* tree. There's a beaut branch comes right down near the summerhouse window, and there's a bit of glass missing. I bust it with my catapult one day. I heard every word, and I never knew a more daft idea.'

Both girls turned pink, then Judith said loftily,
'That's only a male opinion. For men to be impressed
it'd have to be something to do with improving our . . . .
um . . . financial status. To do with money,' she added
explanatorily.

Davy uttered a sound of derision. 'I *know* what
financial status means. Well, it sure was a clunky idea. I
never heard such rubbish! Luenda isn't the soppy kind.
She wasn't keen on Daryl, that's all.'

Luenda looked startled. 'That's quite true. Girls, you
haven't got any ideas about trying to bring us together,
have you? Because it would be nonsense. I'm not in love
with him and he won't break his heart over me. He'll be
up here . . . we'll be in the Far South, and we've never
been more than partners. Now . . . I'll set the table, you
girls get the rest of your homework done upstairs, and
I'll call you when it's ready.

'Davy, you can go down to the shop and get some
hokey-pokey icecream. Straight back with it, mind, so it
doesn't melt. And don't take Griff, even on his lead, the
traffic's heavy.'

She was just finishing pouring the pudding-sauce into
a jug when she saw Davy coming in the gate with a
man. Botheration! Well, whoever it was, she just hoped
he wouldn't stay. They'd never get dinner at this rate.
The corner of the house cut both figures out as they
climbed up. There was an outburst of barking, then a
deep voice acknowledging Davy's introduction of the
stranger to his dog.

Lauenda began to walk towards the back door. It
was pushed open and Davy's voice announced
importantly, 'Luenda, this is the man from the sheep-
station. I met him coming in. It's Gwillym Vaughan.'

It was Gwillym Vaughan, yes, but it was also the man
who had stared at her with such scorn in that all too-
revealing and seductive evening gown!

What a first impression!

CHAPTER TWO

LUENDA summoned the same spurious calm to her aid
as when she had had to appear in that wretched dress.
She looked him straight in the eye, held out her hand,
said, 'Oh, good evening, Mr Vaughan. I wasn't
expecting to meet you till the day after tomorrow. Do
come in.'

He was big, towering in fact, rather hatchet-faced,
and still in the casual clothes. No wonder the trousers
had been creased; he'd have been in them all night, of
course, over the Pacific from Los Angeles.

She led the way into the dining-room, indicated a
chair, and took one herself. She was glad to sit down.
She said, 'Have you been in Auckland all day, Mr
Vaughan?' There was the faintest hint of reproof in her
tone, a sort of why-not-contact-me-earlier question in
it.

'Not really. We were grounded in Nandi, Fiji, for some
hours with engine trouble, so didn't get in till well after
noon. It took a bit of time to get through Customs—it
was a crowded plane. I rang your solicitor, the one the
Californian firm had been in touch with, but he'd gone
out to a client on the North Shore. His secretary wants
me to ring him at his home at eight tonight to see if he
can see me then, privately. Apparently he lives out this
way, so I thought I'd call on the chance of getting you
in.'

Luenda said, 'I thought we were to meet in his office
the day after tomorrow. I've made arrangements with
my employer to have a two-hour lunch break. Must you
do this after hours?'

'I must, otherwise I can't see him. I'm needed at
Mount Serenity. I managed to get a cancellation with
Air New Zealand, but the delay in Fiji made it
awkward to do any business today. I'm taking the

Mount Cook plane from here early tomorrow morning—it goes via Christchurch, Mount Cook, Queenstown. Then I've to get to Ludwigtown and across the lake. Quite a journey.' The dark eyes looked keenly at her from under the jutting brows. What a strong bone formation in his features. 'I had to see you, to try to straighten out this extraordinary situation which you may understand a lot more than I do.'

Luenda made herself say calmly, 'David, I want you to go upstairs to the girls and tell them dinner will be on in twenty minutes' time. You're to stay with them till then.'

When Davy had left the room she turned to this man whose hostility was so marked and said, 'When we did meet, I was hoping *you* might be able to explain some of it to *me*. It's been such a bombshell.'

She was sure there was unbelief in his voice. 'Was it now? I thought it was more in the way of a windfall for you. I thought that when Megan was here, you must really have made the most of your time and that you must know a great deal about our set-up down South.'

So the gloves were off! Luenda could frown too, even if her golden-brown brows weren't as fearsome as his. 'I certainly didn't make the most of anything. She spoke of the loveliness of the lake and the homestead bay, that's all. We talked more about—about a slight connection her family and mine had, long ago.'

She couldn't, to this antagonistic stranger, reveal Gillian's secret. She supposed he'd been staying at Gillian's Californian home. Had Gillian's husband known about Beverley, either before their marriage, or later?

He said: 'A *slight* connection?'

Luenda felt her colour rising. 'Yes, very slight. Not enough to warrant a gesture like this. But it seemed that long ago my grandfather and grandmother did a great service to someone—someone very dear to Megan Richards, and this, it seems, was her way of paying it back.'

He said slowly, 'Gifts aren't usually given with any thought of recompense.'

She showed a spark of resentment. 'There were no

strings attached. I said a service, not a gift. Megan herself didn't know about it till quite recently.' She added quickly, 'And neither did I. But when she told me I was glad, because it brought my grandparents back to me again. I remember them vividly, and they were wonderful people—big-hearted. When my father died, they took my mother and myself in, so Mother could go out to work for us both. It couldn't have been easy, starting off with a young child again, but they never made me feel a nuisance. I liked hearing this about them.'

He nodded, seeming to accept that. Then he said consideringly, 'But I still can't understand this . . . this whim of Megan's to get you to uproot and come down to Mount Serenity, a high-country sheep-station, with only access by boat across an immense lake. A girl from Auckland!'

Luenda said meaningfully: 'Megan was once a girl from Auckland.'

This time the deep-set eyes looked directly at her. 'But she did it for love, not money. She and Evan scratched for an existence in those days, and had few conveniences. No power, no telephone, but a radio receiving-set . . . a launch calling once a fortnight, always at risk if they were ill. Nowadays we get a doctor in by helicopter in emergencies. Megan endured all that for love.'

Luenda's emotions threatened to swamp her. 'Perhaps I'm doing it for love too . . . love of my half-sisters and brother. I can't turn this opportunity down, much as I'd like to. What benefits me benefits them.'

'Can't you?' His lips curled, his eyes swept round the lovely house that was to be theirs for such a short time more. Every room spoke of good taste and the reasonable means that had once been theirs. No doubt he had noticed the double garage, the framework they'd used for painting their launch . . . and imagined an expensive craft bobbing at the shore below. He would know that houses in these bays were very expensive. Words rose to Luenda's lips, but didn't get uttered. She had been going to spill out what their circumstances were, what had brought them to this pass, but he said with a note of real puzzlement in his voice, 'I can't think *why* Megan was persuaded that any abstract and long-ago debt she felt she owed your grandfather had to be paid—in this absurd way—to his granddaughter.'

Persuaded.

Luenda felt a nasty taste in her mouth. If she told him the story he'd think she *had* cried a poor mouth to his employer. That she'd recognised her as owning a valuable country property and had played her cards well. He'd never believe that it was Beverley who had told Megan the sorry tale. Beverley must know Gillian was her mother because when Megan died, Beverley had flown straight across the States to help her. Dear Aunt Beverley, who'd been so concerned when their father had died in such circumstances. But Gillian's husband might not know. To him Beverley might be just a New Zealand friend of his wife's. Besides, she just couldn't face telling this stern-faced man about her stepfather and the gambling. He'd think them all irresponsible, living beyond their means, even shiftless, and grasping meanly at this unexpected windfall. He'd never believe they hadn't used their plight to work on Megan's sympathies.

She lifted her chin. 'Mr Vaughan, is it possible you feel as strongly as this about it because you feel the property and the income from it should have been left entirely to you?'

His look was steady, his tone convincing. 'No. Megan had every right to do as she wished with her money. And I don't—evidently—know all the ins and outs of her personal life. I knew something was to come my way, though I'd hoped it might not for years yet. I loved Megan, I can't even believe she's gone yet. But my expectations weren't wangled for. I felt quite justified in taking something, because I've certainly toiled to make Mount Serenity pay, through good years and poor. I was shocked, I must admit, to find half the income for a year is to go to a perfect stranger, with some weird, rather worrying proviso of more to come at the end of what seems to be a trial year. If I were Megan's sister I'd resent that.'

Luenda flashed back, 'I thought that too, but someone assured me that Megan had earlier made over some holdings into a trust fund for Gillian and her children long ago. I thought that was very nice. She wanted to see them enjoy it in her lifetime. Mr Vaughan, this proposal from Megan's affairs was a bolt out of the blue to me. I didn't ask for it, but it's come. And *I'm coming*. It was Mrs Richard's wish and it intrigues me. To have no expenses for twelve months suits me very well. You have no right to try to influence me not to come. It will be strange at first, especially for the children, but they'll adapt. They have to.'

His lips were a straight line. 'To suit their sister.'

'To suit me,' she agreed tonelessly. 'You can't do a thing about it, so *you'll* have to accept it too, and adapt. It won't be easy for me either, a new way of life, entirely.'

'But very worth while,' he said suavely. She didn't answer. He added with a short laugh that sounded contemptuous to her, 'I wonder if you have any idea what you're letting yourself in for. It's no picnic living at Mount Serenity. We don't carry passengers. You'll have to work, and work hard.'

'I was brought up to work. I'm expecting us to keep our own rooms clean, to help with the cooking, not only for the household but for shearers and seasonal workers. I guess I could even learn to help with farm chores ... if you're patient enough to teach me. You hear of girls working as rouseabouts. Why not me?'

His laugh was maddening. 'I can't see the girl who wore that startling gown this afternoon picking up stinking daggings and tailing lambs.'

Luenda said, 'I'm not a professional model, I'm a secretary. But my boss asked me to model those last few gowns in an emergency, and I'm far too fond of him to refuse.' Then she said sharply, 'What are you looking like that for?'

'Like what?'

'Sardonic would best describe it, I think. Anything wrong in being fond of one's boss? I don't crawl to him, if that's what you think. I know these days employees get up against their bosses very easily, and never see their point of view, never realise they have terrific worries that wage-earners wouldn't care to shoulder ... but my boss is one of the most popular.'

'Very admirable. I'm in favour of that ... if it's not carried to excess.'

She gave it up. 'Look, the children are starting to come downstairs. I don't want *them* to feel they're going where they aren't wanted. Any chance of you doing the decent thing and not showing that? They lost their mother just eighteen months ago, and their father a year later. They're good kids and they're trying to make it easy for me. How about it, Mr Vaughan?'

He said, 'That's the nicest thing that's been said since I came in. I approve. Will do. And to help things along, and seeing we'll be forced into close quarters with each other, to say nothing of sharing isolation, I suggest you call me Gwillym. I'll call you Luenda. Incidentally, I've never heard that name before. Is it one of these fancy invented names?'

She said, scornfully, 'I'd have expected a man with a name as Welsh as yours to recognise another Welsh name. In its original form, my great-grandmother's name was Lluendah ... with two L's, like your own middle name of Lloyd ... and an H tacked on at the end. How about that?'

'I stand corrected and humiliated,' he said, with an irrepressible hint of laughter in his eyes. The next moment the children were piling in.

'We've been awfully good,' said Judith, never one to hide her light under a bushel. 'We were dying to meet Mr Vaughan, but we didn't come down a second under the twenty minutes. Are you staying for dinner, Mr Vaughan? You will, won't you, so we can get to know you?'

He looked uncertainly at Luenda. 'I did stop for a hamburger—all I had time for. I was afraid I might miss you if I left it till after dinner in case you went out. But I realise an unexpected guest at a mealtime can be awkward.'

Luenda came in very quickly. 'Not at all. You must stay. Dinner for four easily stretches to five, not like dinner for two. And with these three voracious appetites, I always allow for second helpings.'

Davy said, beaming on the visitor, 'You're in luck. I picked the pudding tonight—it's a reward for not kicking up a fuss about something. Guess what it is? My favourite ... especially with hokey-pokey ice-cream.'

Luenda had to admit he was prepared to be decent with the children. He said, 'Um ... let me see ... what do boys like best? It goes with icecream. Pavlova filled with fruit salad or kiwi fruit? No? Am I right on the Pav and wrong on the filling? Is it filled with cream and passionfruit?'

Davy squealed with glee. 'Wrong on all counts. You'll have to do better'n that. You're not even hot ... though the pud is.'

'Then it's pie. Apricot pie? Blueberry pie? Apple pie?'
'It's not pie at all.'

'Um ... fruit flummery ... oh no, that's not a hot one. Can you have chocolate mousse hot? I give up.'

'You're way off, Mr Vaughan. It's Christmas pudding with caramel sauce and five-cent pieces and hokey-pokey icecream put on last.'

Luenda grinned. 'Mum and I were never sure if Davy really liked it best or if he had a base financial motive. Sorry it's not a cold dessert on such a hot day, but a promise is a promise.'

Gwillym Vaughan said, 'Never mind, the ice cream cools it down. I'm with young Davy. Steamed puddings are my favourites too. Davy will go down all right with Wilkie. She's scornful of desserts that are so light they disappear like snowflakes in Hell, and feels every girl ought to be brought up to make pies and puds. Just as well we work hard down lake, or we'd be piling on the weight.'

Luenda felt absurdly grateful to Davy ... some feathery concoction would have marked her as unsuitable to cook for farm appetites.

Gwillym Vaughan said, 'You'd better make it Gwill, kids. Like William becomes Bill.'

Luenda served the casserole, thick with vegetables, and put out dishes of mashed potatoes, beaten up with parsley, beans from their own garden and tiny carrots, then the pudding, deftly inserting two coins in Davy's portion, unnoticed by him. It was less of a strain than she had anticipated, simply because the children took over.

They learned that it had been a fourth generation property, till now when Mrs Richards had had no son to inherit. 'Just as well then,' said Judith, rather unfortunately, Luenda thought, 'that someone with a Welsh name like Morgan should fall heir to it. Better to go to a Morgan rather than a Macdonald or an O'Riley, don't you think? And you're a Vaughan.'

Luenda's voice was sharp. 'Judith, there's no question of that. We're given half the income for a year, and that's all.'

Judith looked surprised, then observed shrewdly, 'Bound to be something in it for you at the end of that year, Luenda.'

Luenda said, 'I'm not looking beyond this year, Judy. After that, no doubt, Megan will have made final disposal to those who really deserve it.'

Gwillym looked across at her and said, 'Don't head them off. I find their candour quite refreshing, Luenda. Yes, Judith, that's one bit I like ... the Welsh connection. Tell me, or is it a private matter, what didn't you make a fuss about, Davy?'

'About the fact that Griff mightn't be able to come down to Central Otago right away. He hates kennels. When Luenda went to Nevada we stayed with friends at North Shore and they couldn't have Griff because their dog was too old and too jealous, so we had to board him out, and he fretted like mad.'

Luanda saw a calculating look in Gwillym's eyes and

thought wearily that he probably thought they had
enough money for expensive holidays in the States. She
couldn't bring up the venue of her stepfather's death
now, and here in front of the children.

She thought Gwillym changed the subject quickly.
She was grateful the children asked so many questions.
She was dying to know so many of the answers herself.

. . . Yes, it was true that no roads ran to Mount
Serenity. There were none to Strathdearn on the eastern
side of them, nor to Mahanga-Puke, which meant Twin
Hills, the station to the west, but though they were
miles apart, rough riding tracks led to them and at
least, at night, you could see their lights, and the lights
of Ludwigtown right opposite. But there was more
coming and going than of old, with all the stations
owning big launches.

Miles' and miles of telephone wires now marched
across foothills and rivers and ravines to lessen the
sense of isolation, and great pylons rose above the
skyline to bring them power more reliable than the old
generators each station had had. Though even they
were a great boon after only lamps and candles and
coal ranges.

'But it's still a little world of our own; so much that
you depend upon here just doesn't exist across lake.
There are days in winter when we can't put the boats
across. We keep up tremendous stores of provisions
because at times storms put the power off and break
communication. It's no terrain for softies.'

He was enjoying warning Luenda off, she was sure.
Diana said with relish, 'And of course, apart from tractors,
there'd be no use at all for transport other than horses,
would there? I mean, with no roads it's hardly——'

He said, 'We've fifty miles of a network of roads
within the station itself. Not going anywhere except
back again . . . we have distant huts . . . you could call
them outposts really, on great grazing tracts back in
valleys that are more sheltered than the flats near the
shore. There are huts and yards at all these outposts.
There's a good deal of movement of stock at certain

times. We have cattle, but only dry cattle. Mainly
Herefords, but way back up the roughest gullies, we
have Black Galloways. They're splendid for clearing
land that will later be used primarily for sheep. They
clean up rank tussock, saves us burning it off. They
open up some of the rough blocks so it's suitable for
top dressing from the air. So we have cattle-pens at the
huts as well as sheep-pens.'

Luenda said, 'You said dry cattle. For beef? But I
suppose you have a couple of cows for house use?'

He shook his head. 'We play it lazy these days. The
tourist launch calls twice a week with bread and milk,
bottled and pasteurised—saves a lot of hassle. Very few
people like milking, and separating and scalding. We
can use the men on other jobs. With good refrigeration,
twice a week is adequate. We do keep dried milk on
hand in case of power-cuts. Believe me, the life now is
luxury compared with the long-ago self-supporting
days, though they kept a cowman then, and a man to
make the bread.' He turned to Diana. 'But we use
horses a lot just the same. We do a lot of lower
mustering that way. Not the high-tops, that's all on
foot, it's too steep for horses. We muster to four
thousand feet.'

Di said cautiously, 'Are they all working horses?'

'Do you ride?'

'No, I've always wanted to, but haven't had the
chance. Would—would anyone be able to teach me?
Are there any animals not working?'

'Yes, and some would be the better for exercise.
You're on, Diana.'

Luenda relaxed a little. There wasn't going to be stiff
opposition, then. He was accepting their arrival, even
though inwardly raging at the need to do so. She had a
feeling he hoped it would prove too tough for them,
that they wouldn't stick it out. Would he purposely
make it too hard?

Judith was more diffident. 'I suppose you have
battery cages for your fowls? Because of the produc-
tion.'

'Good heavens, no! We don't sell eggs or poultry. The hens are on free range, and you never saw such a motley lot—Black Leghorns, White Leghorns, Silver Wyandottes, Rhode Island Reds, Sussex, Black Orpingtons, feather-legged bantams, smooth-legged bantams that raise umpteen clutches of chickens by themselves. You name it, we've got it. Are you interested?'

Judith looked starry-eyed. 'I love them. Reared like that, that is.'

'You can have them. They roam all day, so you've got to hunt for the eggs. When the hay-baler's not in use I'm darned if they don't nest in that. We've always meant to organise them better, but we never get round to it—just haven't time. As long as we have enough eggs for the table and cooking, we don't worry. They mostly sleep in the macrocarpa trees. They have perches in the fowl-houses, but they've got minds of our own, our hens.'

'And personalities, probably,' said Judith rapturously.

It was too much for Luenda, and she burst out laughing. 'I'm finding out things about my own sister I'd not dreamed of!'

It was so long since her laughter had been anything but forced, it made her feel better immediately. Presently she said, 'Now, girls, wash the dishes, then upstairs to finish your homework. Mr Vaughan—I mean Gwillym—has to ring Mr Freemont shortly, and I want to do some phoning before then.'

He helped them clear away. It gave Luenda an odd feeling. He hated the thought of their coming, that was evident, yet he was being nice to the children. For the first time she began to feel it might work. And at the end of the year, what? However, meantime it solved their urgent needs. She had a year's grace, a year free of these horrible bills. Anything could happen after that.

The girls went upstairs. Luenda said, 'I'm going to do my ringing from Dad's study. Davy, you can entertain Gwillym. But just small talk, mind. No long spiels about our family history, or pestering him with more questions about Mount Serenity.'

Gwillym Vaughan grinned. 'I think I'm old enough to lead the conversation in the right paths. And we have three small boys on the station ... the oldest about Davy's age, Fergus, Robert, and Duggie. I'm used to all sorts of confidences and I know how to head them off if it's something I think the parents don't want me to know.'

Luanda had to come back into the dining-room to get the telephone book. She heard a small earnest voice, manfully making small talk, say, 'When you lie in bed at night, do you always twine the little toe of your left foot round the little toe of your right foot? I do. I can't stop myself doing it, but I don't know why. Do you?'

Luenda, startled, looked across to the couch. For the first time she saw Gwillym Vaughan's angular face break up completely into laughter. He looked at Luenda without a trace of hostility or reserve. 'Well, you did say small talk, didn't you? ... You can't get it any smaller than little toes, can you? Do you know, David, I believe I do, but I've never realised it till now. I'm sure there must be some deep psychological reason for it. Wouldn't it be interesting if we could work it out? We could be great benefactors to mankind.'

'Yeah. Perhaps it's an embryonic position. Do you think it could be? There was this int'resting programme on T.V. about how babies like to ... um ... revert to the position they knew before birth ... did you see it?'

She saw Gwillym's jaw muscles tighten. He knew boys all right and how they liked to be taken seriously, not laughed at. She went out quickly in case laughter overtook her. She heard Gwill say: 'You could be right. I'll ask our doctor some time.'

She relaxed even more. True, she might not have done had she heard the subsequent dialogue. Davy was still annoyed about the way those girls had behaved this afternoon, shutting him out of their confab and then saying what they had when, all unknown to them, he'd been up the tree.

They'd said he was too young to understand, that boys didn't about those things, anyway, and that in any case he simply didn't have the imagination. That Luenda was an innocent abroad when it came to men. She didn't glamorise herself, but minimised her own charms ... that the men in her life thought she was like a Victorian maiden, wedded to duty, in this case, to the three of them.

If they didn't watch it, she'd finish up an old maid, sacrificed on the altar of family responsibility ... they must boost her with the next man to arrive on her horizon ... she had the looks, she had the charm, only she didn't make enough of either. That it would be a good idea if there were any eligible men on this sheep-station, to endow her with a past simply choc-a-bloc with men!

Davy had thought it a clunky, soppy idea at first, but somehow since he had met this guy Vaughan, he thought there might be something in it. He'd show those girls! This was his chance. Given a bit of a boost, this man who lived on this super place, where real adventures happened season in, season out, Luenda might marry him and they'd never have to leave it.

Davy waded in, surprising even himself. Why, he could beat those girls hollow when it came to imagination!

Luenda rang Mr Freemont, told him what had happened and said that on no account did she want Mr Vaughan to know what had happened to her stepfather. 'He'll think us a feckless lot, spending beyond our means, hopelessly in debt. I'd rather he thought I was money-minded enough to feel I couldn't pass up the chance of some extra and unexpected money.'

'I see your point, but in any case, there's no need for you to feel any qualms about taking this. And I'd like to say something. I'm sure that Mr Vaughan, whatever he feels now, will come to respect you when he gets to know you. From the short time I've known you I've come to respect you, and so will he. I can't imagine you not pulling your weight in whatever situation you find yourself. I know Joe Ackroyd well, and he's told me a few things. You can see me again after Mr Vaughan has gone south and I'll try to make things as easy as possible for you. Has he said much about the set-up?'

'To be fair, he's been good with the children,' Luenda admitted. 'I think he thinks them the victims of a scheming sister who's whisking them out of their settled existence for the sake of filthy lucre and he's sorry for them. Although I feel weak at the knees at the thought of foisting ourselves on that household, I'm determined to go. The housekeeper rules them with a rod of iron, I think. It'll be awful for her having a young strange woman landed on her. It'll be ghastly if she ups and offs to that house in Ludwigtown.'

'My dear, you're meeting trouble halfway. I've a feeling that if it came to that, you'd buckle in and prove your worth. Did anything Mr Vaughan say make you feel this was likely?'

'Just that he's going home sooner because she's not well. He said she's hardly had a day's sickness in her life. I—I've got a feeling she's upset.'

'Then you may be just what she needs ... pitch in and help, but defer to her in everything. Let her feel you aren't assuming the airs of an owner, rather that you're obeying the kindly whim of an eccentric benefactor. I'd like you to write to me when you've been there a week or two. I've become very interested. So has my wife, though she's never met you. Don't write to me as a solicitor, just as a sort of uncle. You can tell Mr. Vaughan he can come whenever he likes. He'd better take a taxi. You can tell him I'll understand he won't want to be too late if he's taking off early and I'll run him back to the hotel at the airport.

'I'll respect your confidence, and it will be as well if, for the present, he doesn't know about your stepfather. I believe it was just the reaction of a heart overburdened with grief. Who can judge? But some do, especially these strong characters. Now, don't lose any sleep over this ... I'm here to watch over your interests.

And . . . God bless!'

The kindness in his voice was almost too much for Luenda. She had to wipe tears away and blow her nose. She returned to the dining-room. 'Thank you, Davy, for entertaining Gwillym. You can have a game with Griff, then run your bath.'

She didn't think she liked the expression on Gwillym's face when he said, as Davy got out of earshot, 'He certainly did entertain, he was even instructive.'

She didn't reply for a moment, and he said sharply, 'What's the matter? Have you been crying? Is there someone you hate to leave? But it's too early for good-byes yet, surely. Or are you finishing with him now?'

She boggled, then said indignantly, 'I don't know what you mean. I only *nearly* cried. It—it was just that Mr Freemont was so sweet to me on the phone it—it got to me. I'm not going to weep all over you. Don't be nervous.'

She thought he looked at a loss. He made an involuntary movement with his hand towards her, then restrained himself. 'You've been speaking to him?'

'Yes.' Oh dear, it sounded sneaky. She said hurriedly, 'It was not far off eight, and I thought you might miss him. He'd been out for dinner and had just got in. He'd like you to taxi over right away, and he'll run you back to your hotel. It's not far. This is Mission Bay. He lives at St. Helier's Bay. I'm sorry we haven't a car left, or I'd run you there.'

Gwillym looked surprised. 'Do you mean you've got rid of the cars already? You *are* in a hurry to go south, aren't you?'

Stung, Luenda retorted, 'That's quite uncalled for. I sold our big car soon after we lost Dad—it was far too heavy on petrol. And though it would have been convenient to keep Mother's, I was offered a very good price for it, cash.'

The brows came down. 'It looks as if I owe you an apology.'

'It does . . . but am I going to get it?'

To her chagrin he chuckled. 'Touché! My mother

would say that's no way at all to offer one. I do
apologise. Now there's something I want to ask before I
go. What was behind saying you might not be able to
bring the boy's dog down right away? Are you wanting
to get rid of it?'

She gave him a levelling look. 'You'll be making
another apology if you go on like this, Gwillym
Vaughan! Have you no imagination? Here am I, a
cuckoo in the nest as far as Mount Serenity is
concerned. What a name, by the way ... it doesn't
sound serene to me. And I've a small brother who
expects to take a pet dog to a sheep-station, and they're
not always welcome. I can't see him as a sheep-worrier,
but it does occur. I was terrified he might be forbidden
to bring Griff. So I wondered if I could board him out
for a few weeks till I'd had time to size up the situation.
And the people I must live with.'

The dark face softened a little. 'Don't you know,
Luenda Morgan, that Corgis have generations of
ancestors behind them who were sheepdogs? I know a
woman who runs a small farm and who depends
entirely on one small Corgi bitch. Griff isn't very old
yet—that's a good point. He'll learn from the others.
He'll be very welcome. You'll have to have a certificate
to prove his injections are up to date, and that his
hydatids record is straight. See to it right away, then
you can fly him down with you. I'll leave you the
number of Mount Serenity. You'll have to ring so you
can be met at Ludwigtown with the launch.

'Get in touch with the Correspondence School in
Wellington immediately you know your arrival date,
and mention to them that the Hemmingways, my
tractor man's children, are with the School. But Mrs
Hemmingway won't be able to add your three to hers.
You'll have to supervise their lessons. There's plenty of
room in our schoolroom. Now I'll get that taxi. I'm
glad he realises I don't want to be late. I still have to
ring Mount Serenity from the hotel to find out how
Wilkie is.'

'Be my guest,' Luenda invited. 'Ring from here now.'

He shook his head decidedly. 'No, I'd prefer to do it later.'

She knew why. He wanted to report on her.

This evening hadn't gone too badly, that wasn't what was worrying her, but the memory of that scornful face watching her in that beautiful, horrible dress did.

Gwillym stood for a moment in silence, and she felt he was considering something. Then he said abruptly, 'There's one thing I *must* say, and I'll make no apologies for *this*. I've got three single young chaps on the station, and a married man. Ours is an isolated community. Unattached women on a place like that can be the very devil. Like governesses, for instance—they can play merry hell. There's not enough love-life for them. That's really why I didn't want you at Serenity. I'm warning you ... I want no feminine mischief made on my patch. Do you understand?'

Luenda didn't think she'd ever been so angry in her life. Cold angry. She said, between her teeth, 'I understand you very well, Gwillym Vaughan. Neither you nor any member of your payroll will have anything to fear from me. Just go. Circumstance has forced us together. All I can hope for is that at the end of the year I must spend at Serenity, I never need to see you again.'

CHAPTER THREE

GWILLYM'S visit had achieved one thing. The girls and
Davy had lost any aversion they might have had
towards pulling up the tent pegs. The news that Griff
could travel on the same plane thrilled them and of
course, Davy most of all. 'He's sure a swell guy, that
one,' he said. Luenda had a vision of things to come.
Davy and his dad had been the best of pals, always
messing about with boats, engines, cars, bikes. Davy
would attach himself to this man. Would that be good
or not? Might there be storms ahead over what could
happen a year hence?

Luenda had no time to agonise over the situation and
got whirled into a dizzying timetable of things to do
with selling the house, of arranging storage for what
they must keep, deciding how many of the children's
things to take. There must be enough to make them feel
at home, poor lambs, but not enough to be a nuisance
to the homestead or cost too much in transport.

At last all was resolved and there came the night
when she must ring Gwillym to tell him the date and
time of their flight. Her knees felt quaky as she picked
up the telephone. She hoped Mrs Wilkins might answer.
That way she might gain some idea of her personality
and if they were welcome or not.

Her luck was out, for Gwillym answered. Oddly,
when she wasn't face to face with him, that beaky man
with the formidable brows, she found his voice
charming, with that slight upward lilt betraying his
Welsh ancestry. If she had thought he might have
mellowed in the interval, though, she was mistaken. He
was bowing to the inevitable, but that seemed all.

'You're ringing to give me a date, perhaps? I can only
hope——'

She cut him off. 'I am. I've booked. If it doesn't suit

you to come across for us, we can take the tourist launch. We can put up in Ludwigtown till the day it runs.'

'Of course I'll be over to get you. Three children, you, Griff, and a mountain of luggage, I daresay.'

'Well, luggage for four,' she made her tone sound sweetly reasonable. 'And you did tell me to bring the children's treasures so they're not too wretchedly homesick. There are a lot of books, but I shouldn't imagine it would be beyond the capacity of the tourist launch. You said they provide a service to the over-lake dwellers, and even take carcases of deer aboard. I let Easter get over, knowing they'd be crowded then. We're on the Mount Cook line and land at Frankton airport early afternoon. How long will it take us to get from Queenstown to Ludwigtown? Then you could just meet us at the wharf.'

He gave a short unamused laugh. 'And how do you think you're getting from Queenstown to Ludwigtown? It's not like Auckland, you know, with buses plying hither and thither. I'll have to arrange for someone with a station-wagon to pick you up. *Would* all your gear go in a station-wagon?'

Luenda took exquisite pleasure in saying: 'I've got that arranged for, Gwillym. After all, it's up to me to cause as little disruption of your farming routine as possible. We have friends who have a holiday house in Queenstown and it so happens they'll be up there that weekend. He used to be our doctor. They've got a station-wagon and a car so they'll have more than enough room. Their name, by the way, is MacCormack—Justin and Barbara MacCormack. If you can give me a time we'll be there, provided the plane's on time. You'd better check before you set out. You know the tag: "If you've time to spare, go by air."'

Once he'd agreed, with a slight note of surprise that gratified her, she went on to ask how Mrs Wilkins was.

'Much better now. She'd had an attack of shingles—fortunately a mild one. She seemed to have been run down. She's a great scout. Of course first of all she'd had everything to do, with Megan being away so long, then Megan's death was a great shock to her. But she had none of the complications that sometimes occur.'

He paused, went on, 'I wanted her to take time off at her daughter's in Invercargill; she has a flat there, but Wilkie said not likely.'

A pause. Luenda said clearly, 'You mean because we're coming? Sorry about that, but I can only hope she'll allow me to help.'

She put the phone down and carried a heavy heart for the rest of the day. Not a promising set-up.

Joe Ackroyd was kindness itself. He and his wife insisted that the family spent their last night with them. Mrs Ackroyd even took the three children and Griff for the whole day to let Luenda see to leaving the house in perfect order for the people who had bought it and who were so tired of temporary quarters they were moving in right away. They'd bought the carpets, the curtains, and some of the furniture, so it still had some dear familiarity for Luenda. But with their parents' photographs packed, their china, pictures, the soul of the house had departed.

What happiness this house had known! Luenda ran a hand lovingly down the banister rail ... memories almost swamped her. As she stepped into the hall, the front-door bell rang.

As she opened it, she saw a lovely girl, a rose-red girl, with a complexion anyone could envy, with shining black hair, a complete contrast to Luenda's thick swirling straw-coloured locks. She had a Highland look, with those deep blue eyes. She said, 'Luenda Morgan? I wanted to meet you before I take off for Australia. I'm from the Lake of the Kingfisher.'

'Oh ... *Lake Moana-Kotare?* Yes, it's a pretty translation, isn't it? How lovely, do come in. I can still offer you a chair because the people who've bought the house retained a few things.'

The girl took a great interest in the surroundings. 'What a beautiful home! What a shame you're leaving it. But of course you could hardly be expected to pass up a chance like that. It must have been like winning a lottery.'

'Not quite. You buy a ticket for that. This came as a *complete* surprise.'

The girl nodded. 'Did it? Yes, I suppose so. That's what I keep saying to Gwill . . . that you couldn't blame anyone for taking it on . . . you'd never dream how many lives could be affected by it. By the way, my name's Fenella Newbolt.'

Luenda went warily. 'Do you live at Mount Serenity? I mean, is your father on the estate or——'

'No, I was at Twin Hills as governess to the younger children. We—I saw quite a lot of the folk at Mount Serenity—by launch. But sometimes I rode over on the track—a long way, but worth it. I loved Serenity. It seemed obvious then that Wilkie and Megan would retire to Ludwigtown before long, so it seemed ideal. But that all changed when Megan died in America. I'm going back to Australia now.'

The beautiful blue eyes looked at her with a sadness that hurt Luenda. Fenella hesitated, then put out her hands, caught Luenda's in them and said passionately, 'Don't tell Gwill I've come, will you? And keep what I'm going to tell you completely confidential. Gwill naturally thought that in time the estate would come to him. But the way it is now, he just couldn't expect a wife to live with another woman, could he, a woman and three children? It just wouldn't work. I felt I must go away till the dust settled.'

Luenda felt appalled. No wonder Gwillym Vaughan didn't want her at Mount Serenity! Fenella sat without saying another word, to give her time to recover. Luenda finally said, 'This has been a shock. I'd no idea it would throw such a mighty spanner into the works. Mr Vaughan gave me no hint. No wonder he was hostile!'

Fenella said slowly, 'He wouldn't—there's too much at stake. He's really slaved at Mount Serenity. He was there before Mr Richards died. Megan couldn't have managed without Gwill then. It was Mr Richards' idea

that Gwill should carry on the estate. He planned that
when Megan should retire, Gwill should have it, that
she would live on the income from half the estate, then
when, in time, Megan died too, it would all be Gwill's.'

The thick black lashes swept upwards to look at
Luenda and saw apprehension and dismay. 'I expect
that half will be yours eventually, now. I'm pretty sure
an earlier will left the lot to Gwill.'

Luenda felt like the usurper in an old-time drama.
What could she say to this girl who obviously loved
Gwill? For whom this situation had shattered a dream.

Tears of sympathy and guilt rushed to Luenda's own
eyes. She reached over and took the hand lying listlessly
in the pale blue lap, 'Fenella . . . it's a horrible situation
for you, for me, for Gwillym. I think I should explain
my own position. Mrs Richards left me what she did
because my grandparents had long ago done someone
she loved a great service. When she was in California
she heard from a mutual friend of the death of my
stepfather. Also that because of the circumstances of his
death we had suffered a severe financial loss.

'I didn't tell Mr Vaughan this, but I'll tell you and
you'll understand. why I had to take advantage of this
unexpected solution to my problems. I loved my
stepfather dearly, but he went to pieces when Mother
died. He began to travel and, unknown to us, to
gamble. He gambled in a big way, from Monte Carlo to
Las Vegas. After the last deadly run of ill-luck he had a
fatal heart attack. We've sold everything, but what's left
after the debts are paid isn't enough for four of us to
live on when even our home had to go. So I can't turn
down a year free of expense.

'I can't do anything about it, Fenella, except ask you
to be patient and mark time for a year. I've no idea
what will happen then, nor has anyone else. It seems
there are sealed instructions. I'm to regard the income
from half the estate as ours. It gives us a roof over our
heads too. After that I've no idea what Mrs Richards
had in mind.'

Fenella's eyes seemed to search hers. 'Haven't you?

Haven't you *really*? Did she drop no hint? Didn't she talk a lot about Gwill? Didn't she try to sell him to you?'

Luenda's tone was bewildered. 'I can't see the drift of this. She never——'

Fenella shrugged. 'I might as well admit that Mrs Richards didn't like me—in fact she hated me. It hurt. I've heard of possessive mothers, but she could undo them all. I thought at first it was a case of not wanting Gwill to marry anyone, that she was afraid of a wife making changes in the homestead. You know how it is, people her age get set in their ways.'

Luenda nodded, and Fenella plunged on. 'But it was more than that. She loathed me. I can't think why ... I tried to please her ... unless she was afraid I couldn't stand the winters and might take him back to Australia. She did all she could to break up our growing attachment. I think when she came here...' the girl paused as if she didn't like to go on.

It was effective. Luenda urged her to go on.

'Please don't be hurt by it, or think I resent you. I can see you're the victim of circumstances as well as I am. She'd tried once or twice to bring in counter-attractions—girls at Ludwigtown, the kind she could have managed. Then she met you, and seemingly got carried away by the fact that she felt she was in debt to your family, and because she was a sick woman, though it didn't develop till she was in the States, she got the idea of bringing you to Serenity if anything happened to her before she could return. There are people who want to rule other people's lives, even from the grave.'

Luenda stared. 'You mean ... you mean match-making?'

'I do. I'm as certain of that as I'm certain of my own presence here. More than matchmaking, which is sometimes no more than a nudge in the right direction; I think she's still pulling strings—or will in a year's time. Everything's in its favour. The upkeep of three children is a big hurdle for a girl. That sealed envelope could, cunningly, offer you a solution. I'm practically certain that when the year is up, you'll be offered half the estate in your own right if you marry Gwill.'

Luenda fell back in the depths of the lazy-boy rocker, said, 'That's ridiculous!' But the look in Fenella's eyes made her wonder the moment after. She stirred uneasily, then said, 'Is it possible?'

'Not only possible, probable.'

Luenda said, snatching at a straw, 'But she never as much as mentioned Gwill. She said she had a good manager on the estate so she had no worries about being away for some months.'

Fenella said slowly, 'That was quite cunning . . . and in keeping. So you'd not guess, if she invited you down there, that she had plans for you.'

All of a sudden Luenda, to her own amazement, heard herself laughing, and there was real merriment in it. 'This has its funny side, Fenella. Even if in a year's time, something like that is revealed, he'd certainly never look *my* way. Believe me, we detested each other on sight. That was why I couldn't face telling him what my stepfather had done, that he'd suffered such a change in character. I couldn't bear this man who was so antagonistic towards me sitting in judgment on Dad. I felt Gwillym Vaughan would never have known how overwhelming grief can be to some people. He might have thought us all tarred with the same brush . . . feckless people, always in debt. Ready to grab any chance of money coming to them.'

Fenella looked relaxed suddenly. 'I feel better now. I—I've regained some hope. It may come out right yet.'

Luenda said compassionately, 'You must cling to that hope. I can't see Gwillym giving up hope either. Won't he just mark time too?'

Fenella bit her lip. 'I'm afraid we quarrelled fiercely over it.'

'In what way? I don't want to pry, but if I know a little, I might be able to ease the situation.'

Fenella said slowly. 'First of all, before we knew about you but had heard about Mrs Richard's death, it seemed to me that Wilkie just wanted to stay on with

Gwill. You see, Mrs Richards had always wanted her as a companion and housekeeper because she herself was always outside, in the saddle or the stockyards—as good as a man. Mrs Wilkie had reigned supreme in the house, and now could more than ever. She certainly doesn't want me there, she has a thing about Australians.'

Luenda's brows came down. 'That sort of thing I can't stand. I loathe people saying: "I don't like the French!" or "I can't stand Italians," and so on. There's no reason in it. People are people. I've a Welsh ancestry and feel an affinity with other folk who have, but I've known some Welsh people I didn't like ... simply because I wouldn't have liked *them*, whatever nationality they'd been. But to dislike people because of that, or because of the colour of their skin, or the fact that they were once enemies of ours, is pure rot.'

'I know. But I suffered because of that.'

Luenda was considering the problem. 'Must you leave this homestead where you've been governess? You aren't on the doorstep, I know, but you're not entirely cut off. If you went back, and came visiting, and if it could be seen we were becoming friends, mightn't it make a difference? Mightn't you and Gwill both feel it could work out—I mean, with us living there? I'm a bit hazy on the set-up, but it sounds large. Couldn't it be divided up so that you and Gwill had quarters of your own, even if, at the end of the year, I have to stay on?'

Fenella grew restless, almost as if she was reluctant to say more, then she burst out with it. 'I don't think you know what that place means to Gwill. I can't help loving him, even though I know how ruthless he is. He'll do anything to be the owner, the sole owner of the Station. He's scared of that surprise packet in the custody of the Queenstown solicitor. If—if there's anything in it like I fear, like *he* fears there is, I think he'd persuade himself his feelings have changed.'

Luenda's eyes grew wide. 'You mean ... you think ... that if in any way pressure was brought to bear upon him, he might ... he might ... no, it's preposterous! Besides, it's also impossible. I wouldn't marry a conniving man like that if he was the last man on earth—sorry about that; evidently he's the man *you* love,' she added hastily. 'But believe me, he'd have no hope with me. You can set your mind at rest on that.'

The hair had swung over Fenella's face like a curtain, hiding her eyes, but now she looked up with every sign of alarm. 'Luenda, you wouldn't get carried away by your anger and tell him this, would you? I'd feel so humiliated. Look, I'll promise not to tell him about your stepfather if you promise not to tell Gwill I called. He knows my Sydney address. If he wants me he'll write to me. Promise?'

'That's easy,' said Luenda recklessly, because she was so incensed against Gwillym Vaughan, and not only on her own behalf. 'I'll promise. Now, we're going to have some coffee—I've got just four biscuits left! You can go off with an easy mind on that score. I've a feeling that things, eventually, will turn out well for you ... if you really want to marry such a man!' The next moment she was saying, 'Oh, I shouldn't have said that!'

Fenella said slowly, 'You have to experience a thing like that before you can hope to understand it. I love Gwill, with all his faults. Even the one that is separating us, his obsession with the land.'

Luenda said soberly, 'I've never owned any land in my own right. If ever I do I hope it doesn't take me that way. It's people who matter. Fenella, it may even be that in a year's time I'll be told it was an experiment to find out if I liked the high-country life, that I'll have given it a go, and if I don't want it permanently, I can have a legacy and come back to Auckland.'

'Is that what you hope for?'

'I expect so. I was brought up in the semi-tropical heat of Auckland, I revel in boating, water-skiing, wind-surfing. I happen to be one of the toughies who has a dip every day, summer and winter. Moana-Kotare is snow-fed, I believe.'

'It is. You'll find it mighty cold. There's already snow

on Mount Serenity in early autumn.'

'See . . .' Luenda spread out her hands, 'play a waiting game. I predict that I'll be back here in twelve months time and you'll be Fenella Vaughan, with Wilkie safely installed in Ludwigtown. Now, let's have that coffee!'

Apart from now feeling terrified about Mrs Wilkins' reaction to another woman in the house, Luenda had little time to brood. Heavens, if she didn't want a wife of Gwillym's in the house, how would she react to an unattached girl with three children under her feet all day? Luenda felt sick, then snapped down her dreads like a blind. What couldn't be changed had to be endured. By tomorrow morning, seeing they were taking the D.C.10 from Auckland to Christchurch at ten past eight, she'd be on her way. And the packing must be finished by then, and those excited children in bed reasonably early at Ackroyds' place.

At last they were soaring up into the clouds, with a last glimpse of the huge city with its twin harbours disappearing into a white, formless world of vapour. Then the cloud ceiling became the floor, and an unmarred canopy of blue was above them, with bright sun striking on the wings.

The children were loving it, and with a delightful hostess assuring Davy that she had first-hand knowledge that a certain little Corgi was taking to the air as if he were the airline mascot, they gave themselves up to the delights of a new experience . . . leaving the North Island for the South Island they had never seen.

By the time they were over the Taranaki Province, every vestige of cloud was gone, and the perfect cone of Mount Egmont stood out against the curved coastline. They got a wonderful view, as they neared Wellington, of Kapiti Island lying like a pendant on a blue satin bosom, before they saw the high-rise buildings and harbour shipping that was the capital; then, magic of magic for the children, Cook Strait, that fearsome stretch of water, world-famous for its storms, and the fretted outline of the Marlborough sounds, with a myriad indentations and the long curve of Farewell Spit marking the north-west tip beyond Nelson.

Davy was awed by the Kaikouras which, from this height, did look frighteningly remote and unexplorable ... 'I thought they were just a thin line, a range, running back to join the Alps, Luenda. And gosh, will you just look at those rivers?'

She nodded, 'All rushing to the Pacific on the East Coast. You can see now what a narrow strip the province of the West Coast is, bordered by the Tasman, between us and Australia. But when we get to our destination, we'll be really inland, at the back of a great lake hollowed out in the Ice Age by a huge glacier ... and we'll be tucked right in among mountains. Mrs Richards told me that Mount Serenity is an illusionary mountain. Some trick of distance or atmosphere makes it appear as if it belongs to other stations, to Strathdearn and Glen Airlie, but it really belongs to Mount Serenity Station.'

'To *us*,' said Davy, with great satisfaction.

'Well, to us for this year, Davy lad, in that we'll live there for that time, but also to Gwillym Vaughan. You won't forget that, will you?'

'Well, I meant him in the "us",' he said impatiently. 'He's sort of family now, isn't he? We'll be living together.'

The by now familiar sensation of butterflies in the stomach descended upon Luenda again. The pastoral checkerboard of the Canterbury Plains drew their attention, with the Cashmere Hills and Lyttelton Harbour guarding the city, and the Alps a silver divide sixty miles west. Then they were descending.

They were amazed to find it so hot as they crossed the tarmac in a blustering wind. 'This is their famed and dreaded Nor'-Wester, I suppose,' said Luenda, getting hurried along by it.

The three children vied with each other to inform her that it was because it had lost all its rain on the Alps as it crossed from the Tasman, then they were into the

terminal building and they were slightly incensed to find
it more luxurious than Auckland Airport. Luenda said
severely, 'Let me warn you here and now, I want no
odious comparisons. I've never liked the rivalry
between the North and the South Islands. We're all
New Zealanders, whichever side of the Strait we were
born. You're going to find it much colder down further,
but I want no grizzles about that. Each island has a lot
to offer. One has a warmer climate, the other has
scenery on a grander, more spectacular scale. You'll
make yourselves unpopular if you draw comparisons,
and I'd like harmony.'

'But you're getting Serenity!' shouted Davy, and was
so overcome with his own wit he stopped worrying
about the transfer of Griff.

'Doesn't seem possible it's only a quarter-past eleven
and that by night-time we'll be in a new home without
even a road coming to the door,' said Judith, with
relish.

Luenda knew flutterings again, but said crisply, 'Now,
over to the Mount Cook Airline counter. There's not a
lot of time to get our seat numbers. No, Davy, of
course there isn't time to visit the cafeteria. Mrs
Ackroyd gave me a packet of goodies, though it
seems incredible, after all you stowed away on the
plane, that you can possibly chew, let alone swallow.
Our call will come soon, and we'll be airborne at twenty
to twelve. Just think, by twelve-thirty you'll be seeing
Mount Cook, all twelve thousand feet of it!'

'Twelve thousand, three hundred and forty-nine,'
said Davy, always a stickler.

They landed a number of tourists at Mount Cook,
which was a glorious sight with not even a tiny cloud to
veil its majesty, and took others on board for
Queenstown. It was hard to imagine the trip would
have taken them five days by car. The farms below
seemed frighteningly distant from each other, though
most at least had roads leading to them.

After the lush green of the North Island it was
strange to see great bare tawny-gold hills, with huge

outcrops of rock thrusting through, gashed by gorges and reflecting blue water deep in them. Two lakes lay beneath them, with just a neck of land separating them, 'Lake Wanaka and Lake Hawea,' the voice on the intercom. informed them, 'and the bluish-green ribbon you see twisting away from Wanaka is the Clutha River, the fifth fastest in the world. On your left you ought to be able to see the confluence of two rivers where the Kawarau which drains Lake Wakatipu joins the Clutha. The junction is below the town of Cromwell, soon to lie beneath power project waters. Now we're losing height to come into Frankton, serving Queenstown, one of the scenic gems of the world.'

What an incredible lake, sapphire blue and shaped like a dog-leg, deep in the trough of towering peaks, jagged and perpendicular, the Remarkables. They had a swift impression of an Alpine town, nestling among larches and pines, then they were down on ground level on a primitive-looking airfield, descending the gangway, and there were the MacCormacks, with their three teenage children, and not far off, the car and station wagon. And it was only ten past one!

Barbara hugged Luenda. 'It's going to be lovely having you here. We come up as often as Justin can get away. You can take a break from over-lake, when you pine for shops and streets ... if you do ... couldn't think of anything more idyllic, myself. I've been on the phone to Gwillym Thingamy, and told him this. He can't pick you up till four, so we're taking you off for lunch at our place. We're on the road to Queenstown, and it's no great distance to Ludwigtown.'

The Doctor went off with Davy, to collect Griff, and they all laughed as the air-crew patted him goodbye. He pranced along, greatly excited, on his lead. In ten minutes they were turning down a steep drive from the road, and Luenda was surprised to find the gradient suddenly level out to a crested terrace to where a double garage formed part of the house that was built over the almost sheer bank below. 'This gives us a superb view,' exulted Dr Justin. 'We look across to Cecil and Walter

Peaks on one side and the Remarkables on the other. See . . . over to the left.'

Luenda drank it in, finding great comfort in the immensity of it. 'Oh, Doctor, I've been so dreading being away from the sea! I've always been within sight and sound of it, and thought I might feel claustrophobic hemmed in by land and hills . . . but if there is this, I can take it. Is Moana-Kotare like it?'

'Yes, smaller, but not small, lass, and blue-green like the colour of a kingfisher instead of sapphire. A fascinating place. Now, if you've gazed your fill, let's eat. Barbie has it all ready.'

Luenda felt an immense gratitude. The MacCormacks would be up often enough to be a refuge for them if life with that dark-visaged Welshman at Serenity proved too grim to take, week in, week out.

While they ate their bacon-and-egg pie and their salads, the Doctor said, 'Sensible fellow, that Gwillym Vaughan. He rang me in Dunedin three days ago, said he'd just discovered people can pick up chickenpox from someone with shingles, and wondered if he should allow you to bring three children into that risk. He thought you might like to stay on in Auckland till danger of infection was over. I told him to my certain knowledge, seeing I was then the family doctor, that the four of you had had chickenpox five years ago. Very considerate of him, don't you think?'

Luenda agreed, though her private judgment was that any delay in their arrival would have been welcome news to Gwillym Vaughan.

They piled into the car and wagon and set off through Queenstown, crossing the Shotover River by the Edith Cavell Bridge where the poplars were so bright they almost hurt the eyes, threaded through valley flats beneath Coronet Peak, so beloved by skiiers from all over the world, and so came the Ludwigtown on the shores of the Lake of the Kingfisher. They were there in loads of time, to Luenda's relief. They piled their belongings out . . . what an array! But when they were coming here to live, it was stupid to feel guilty.

Justin said, 'This will be him,' as they saw a sizeable launch come into view from the far waters, white against its blue-green.

Luenda, used to boats all her life, could see he handled it well. He was in blue jeans, with a light blue and navy sweater pulled over them, and he wore a peaked cap that gave him a nautical air and she noticed, reluctantly, that it did things for his profile. He was a quite handsome man really. She pulled herself up on the thought. Well, when he wasn't scowling, that was.

No one could have guessed it was other than a greeting to people he was pleased to welcome. Perhaps he was impressed that she had friends like Justin and Barbara. He came off, said a comprehensive hullo, bent first to fondle Griff's head, then Davy's. 'He stood up to the journey all right, Davy? And I guess he's used to boats.' Introductions followed. He even said, 'Next time you're in Queenstown, come across on the tourist launch, then I'll run you back, after a day with us. Nice for Luenda if you can do that.'

He was even affable about that luggage. 'You managed jolly well if this is the sum total of your baggage.' Iain and Donald and their father helped stow it, a man belonging to the wharf loaded drums of fuel aboard and stores. The big moment was upon them. When they cast off, they would be bound for a new life, isolation and, possibly, problems.

Justin, Barbara and Nonie kissed them all fondly . . . the boys were still in raptures over the launch . . . then they were on. Griff barked furiously from where he was tied. Gwill started the engine and they headed across the lake.

The children kept him busy identifying headlands, homesteads, an island or two, shipping buoys, asking questions as to the depth of the lake—a fearsome one— the temperature in winter, in summer . . . what fish there were, what birds frequented the shores. Well, the Sherbornes were like that. Any ignorance of theirs was certainly not caused by diffidence. The questions fairly tumbled out.

Luenda said, coming closer to the wheel, 'Feel free to tell them to shut up if you prefer to concentrate. They'll take it.'

The brows came down. 'I hope you've not made me out an ogre, in the crusty bachelor image.'

The children were with Griff now, so she said in a low tone, 'Not to them. The thought crossed *my* mind, though, that you could be just that. But I've made up my mind to be tolerant. It isn't easy for you in any way. Your quiet life has been disrupted and no doubt it has caused a multitude of financial complications. But I gave away nothing of my fears to them.'

Gwillym turned his head which brought his face close to hers. To her surprise he grinned, his eyes looking directly into hers. 'Then at least I start off on the right foot with them. I thought I might have a barricade to break down there.'

Luenda felt a burning blush spread from her throat. She said quickly, 'I'm sorry. I've been so wrapped up in my own reactions I didn't think of you having dreads too. I can't think of anything worse than having your home invaded by three children who might resent you. If it eases your mind at all, they think you're a great guy. They may be homesick and may play up if it gets them badly when the novelty wears off, but when you made it easy for them to bring Griff, they were pro-Gwillym Vaughan there and then.'

His eyes crinkled with amusement. 'And you? Did it soften you?'

She tightened her lips. 'It could have, but the effect was lost when you warned me not to make mischief among your men.'

He said nothing, and she wished it unsaid. As one might ignore an outspoken child, he said, after the marked pause, making a sweep of his arm, 'In a few moments Mount Serenity will come into view and we'll go round that headland into the most beautiful bay of all. Which is a piece of conceit you'll hear repeated by the MacQueens, the MacCorquodales and the Campions, of *their* bays.'

Luenda was grateful for a safer topic. 'The whole lake is beautiful, and its surroundings. How satisfying to find the water really is the colour of a kingfisher. Fascinating!'

He nodded. 'And always changing. At times, near the lake shore and in certain moods it takes on a sheen like the rings on a peacock's tail, or the colour of the Clutha as seen from the air. Did you notice it?'

'Yes, it snaked out from Lake Wanaka like that hair-ribbon of Diana's. Gloriously colourful against those tawny hills.'

'I thought this landscape might strike you as rather grim and frightening. The North is so gentle and támed.'

'Where we live, yes,' Luenda agreed. 'But not all of it. Some of the dense forest land and ranges of the Central Highlands or around Lake Waikaremaana can be quite intimidating.'

Gwillym looked at her curiously. 'You said that with feeling. Any experience of it?'

'Yes, Dad and I did a great deal of tramping on our own. Mother wasn't keen, and the children were too young. I mean my stepfather, not my own father. We were lost once in the Urerewas ... fortunately we weren't missed so we didn't involve the search and rescue folk, and we never told Mother. It was hard not to panic, but Dad had done a survival course which stood him in good stead. I'll never forget how every forested hill, every gully and stream looked alike. It taught me a lot, though.'

His eye appraised her. 'Perhaps we won't have a tenderfoot on our hands after all. In fact you could even be an acquisition.' It was amazing how that hawklike face softened when he wasn't being hostile. Luenda felt two emotions, the second following very quickly on the heels of the first. One was a surge of hope that the antagonism that had flared so quickly between them might not last, the second, quenching that hope, was the sudden remembrance of Fenella, who in spite of all, loved this man, but had said he loved the land so much he could be expected to do anything to acquire it. Was this a genuine change of feeling, or had he already judged it to be expedient to change his tactics just in case, at the end of that year, she might own part of the property?

She turned about and the headland that had a buoy set at the very point of it had been passed, and the next moment all of them were entranced as the spectacular view burst upon them. It was so symmetrical, so classically beautiful, it could have been a piece of stage scenery.

There was a wide sweep of lake-beach embraced by the sheltering arms of twin headlands, a scarlet jetty, doubled by its reflection, fingering out into the waters. Small white craft bobbed at their moorings and above the cluster of farm buildings the wide-set homestead was surrounded by a mass of trees, native and exotic, with the garden a splash of colour on its many terraces. Above it rose Mount Serenity, as perfectly coned as Mount Egmont, in fact a miniature Fujiyama. Behind it the sunset was painting the sky with a prodigality of flame and coral and gold and amber that was splendour beyond belief.

Luenda said, 'It's like a Technicolor spectacular . . . almost a magic. I feel it's been put on especially for us, to make us welcome.'

Her eyes swept up to the weatherbeaten face over the wheel. Gwillym's voice was expressionless. 'You weren't expecting a welcome, were you?'

She kept her voice low, matter-of-fact. 'It would have been too naïve to expect one, considering the circumstances.'

She hadn't seen him at a loss before. She felt that words he couldn't utter trembled on his tongue. Finally he said, 'Some impacts are too startling. One can be stunned. One can react too quickly. Like coming over the brow of a hill and looking directly into the rays of the sun. You can't see the road ahead for a while, then your sight adjusts. I admit I was appalled when that Californian lawyer came to see us at Megan's sister's place, but now I'm seeing things differently.'

It ought to have been comforting, but it wasn't. Luenda knew it for expediency. There would be rocks ahead.

She decided not to comment and said instead, 'Is that where the fifty miles of roads go, into that valley? Where they reach and come back again?'

'They wind round into another valley, very sheltered, then come back along the shoreline. A track, only fit for tramping, or horses, leads off from it and goes to Strathdearn, our nearest neighbour. It takes half a day riding. There are two big houses there, an old one, the original, and one ranch-house style, very modern. A sister and brother, each married, with their respective partners, live on that property—a big estate, like ours. Only it's always belonged to that family. Not like this, a family depleted by two wars and mishaps, and with the last of the Richards having no offspring. A pity.'

Luenda found herself saying: 'But at least there's a Welshman to carry on. I expect that meant something to Megan, for her husband's sake.'

'Yes, she said so. I wish I'd given her, in her lifetime, what she longed to see—my sons, or daughters, growing up here. However, one marries to please oneself, not other people.'

'I should think so. I'd never marry for less than what my mother married for . . . first with my father, then with Tony. For love. I don't believe in expedient marriages, or for companionship, or to—to amalgamate business concerns or thrones.'

He glanced at her briefly but searchingly. 'You said that with great feeling. What occasioned that, Luenda Morgan? Did someone ever try to persuade you to settle for less?'

She'd been too vehement. She said lightly, with a laugh, 'No, I wasn't speaking from personal experience, just that I heard of someone recently who was weighing up the pros and cons. In this case, material advantages.' She avoided looking at him lest her scorn show in her eyes. 'Oh, is that a clock on that building to the right of the homestead?'

'Yes, a clock tower on the stables. More often seen in Britain than here, but the first Richards, in 1860, followed the old style. It keeps perfect time to this day. When we come about a bit you'll see the other two houses. One is fairly old, like ours, and in marvellous condition, the other newish, bungalow-type, easily kept. It houses old Dick ... his name's Claude, I believe, but as his last name's Turpin, he never gets called anything but Dick. He was here when I first started coming to Serenity for school holidays. Here long before that too. He was the packy on the station then ... the man with the packhorses when they were off mustering at the mountain huts. He'd cook for them. He still looks after the horses and cooks for the three single fellows. A real character, fine if he takes a fancy to you, an old devil if not.'

Luenda decided she'd keep the children well out of Dick Turpin's way. Now they could see quite a bunch of figures on the jetty. Gwillym groaned, 'I knew they wouldn't be able to resist it! They're all there, every man-jack of them. Only Mrs Hemmingway and her brood are missing.'

Luenda's eyes were keen. 'Isn't that Mrs Hemmingway?'

He laughed. 'You mean the tall, elegant one with the bright hair? That's Wilkie. Not everyone's idea of a housekeeper, is she? But she's a terrific one just the same.'

Luenda moved away to restrain the children, though they were too used to boats to be too eager and foolhardy. But Griff was all excitement and noise. She quietened him down.

She straightened up, tall and slim in emerald green trews and top, a brown triangular scarf knotted at her throat, short blonde hair streaked with darker gold blowing back in the wind offshore, with the light from the sunset, tender as it paled, full on her.

At that moment a hearty wolf-whistle burst from

someone in the back of the group—one of the single workers, she supposed. They all laughed as Luenda blushed fierily and a voice, from the elegant housekeeper, said, 'Now, Wayne, give over. That's no way to greet the stranger in our midst!'

Luenda felt very much that. The stranger in their midst.

CHAPTER FOUR

EVEN as she felt very much the incomer in a tightly-knit community, isolated and vulnerable, another voice, presumably this Wayne's, said, 'Have a heart, Wilkie darling! Things like this don't happen every day of the week at the back of beyond ... I'm sure our Miss Morgan will only take it as a compliment.'

Mrs Wilkins chuckled. 'You could be right, you cheeky devil—after all, nothing does as much for a girl's morale as a wolf whistle now and then!'

An involuntary chuckle escaped Luenda, but a quick glance told her Gwillym wasn't smiling. Oh dear. Then, amazingly, Davy said, with a most impish grin, 'What do you mean, Mrs Wilkins? My sister is used to *millions* of wolf-whistles!'

Luenda yelped, 'Davy, what on earth do you mean? Don't be absurd!'

Wayne's voice was admiring. 'And modest with it too. Miss Morgan, we're not half glad to have you here.' He snapped his fingers. 'What do you say, boys?'

As one voice they came in on their cue, 'And so say all of us!'

Their boss's voice was derisive. 'Well, now we've got the fanfare over, how about a hand with the luggage, chaps?'

'Introductions first,' said one of them. 'I'm Dan Porter, and this is my brother Steve, and the cheeky devil is Wayne Lester. But we're doing it wrong ... this is the most important person at Serenity, our Wilkie. She rejoices in the beautiful name of Mirabel, so why we make it Wilkie, I don't know.'

Mirabel Wilkie suited her beautiful name. There must have been Viking ancestors somewhere. Her eyes were the colour of the waters of Wakatipu, pure sapphire, and before the years had added a few white strands here

and there, her hair must have been a ruddy gold like
sun-ripened wheat. But it was more than that, there was
a bone structure that would make her turn heads to
watch, if she lived to be a hundred years old—high
cheekbones, a classically modelled nose, arched brows, a
serene forehead. And her jawline was exquisite.

She was so unexpected for here; she could have been
a buyer for a cosmetic department, thought Miss
Morgan of Ackroyds. She held out her hands to the
girls, said, 'What honeys . . . this will be just delightful!
It'll be like having my daughters here again.' She
grinned at Davy. 'And having my son here, only perhaps you won't be such a pickle as he was at your age.'

'Don't count on it,' warned Luenda.' After a daft remark like he made just now, I'm wondering if I know my
little brother at all. I can't think what's got into him!'

She heard Judith say something to Diana that she'd
rather like to have heard more clearly. It sounded a
little like: 'But *we* know, don't we? Who'd have thought
it?' However, it was lost in her own greeting to Mrs
Wilkins, who turned to her and said, 'You'll be tired,
Miss Morgan—imagine, all the way from Auckland in
one day! Come along. Boys, bring the cases. I won't be
so cruel as to dismiss you right away. You can have a
cup of tea with us, then you can clear off to your own
quarters.'

They groaned, but began picking up the luggage. 'An
invitation to dinner was the least we'd expected. We'd
even have done the dishes.'

When Luenda had first heard of the Mount Serenity
Station, she'd imagined something vast and bare,
carved out of the trough of the mountains by some vast
sculptor of Nature, eroded by the pitiless force of snow-
waters thawing and falling, sweeping vegetation and
boulders from the mountainsides, but this bay had been
lovingly fashioned, and even then the gracious curves
had been gentled and ornamented by generations of
Welsh mountain men into a beauty that surely must be
sought out by artists.

The background was vast enough, with huge ranges

at the back of Serenity itself, and the foreground had the tremendous sweep of the sparkling waters of the Lake, but the homestead and its garden folded into the valley behind it with an air of nestling, of intimacy.

Stilts, black and white, their legs tucked up behind them like aeroplane wheels folded away, made graceful flights over the water, sounding their alarm cries. Oyster-catchers picked their way along the edge more placidly. They began to take their way along a well-made road, oiled to keep the dust down, up the incline towards the property. Back from the lake beach, partly sandy, partly muddy silt, and shingle, was a fascinating rim of driftwood, then turf and willows.

Next began the multitude of trees that must have been planted through nearly five generations in the last century and a quarter—poplars, oaks, limes, chestnuts, plane trees, birches, all in the russet and gold glory of a New Zealand April. Behind the house waited great pockets of New Zealand bush, dense and green; what a place to explore! Luenda's heart lifted. A glorious setting for children.

They came to a lovely drystone wall, made of the lake boulders. Wide gates were pushed back on the inside and looked as if they hadn't been closed for years. She said so as she exclaimed over the workmanship of the wall.

Wilkie said, 'That belonged to the old days when there was one family after another here. The little children had to be kept from straying to the lake. We do shut them when people bring toddlers to stay. Megan was a great one for entertaining. I've a daughter getting married in September, so perhaps those gates will be in use before long. She lives in Invercargill.'

That didn't sound as if Wilkie were planning an early retirement. The ground rose, the trees stood back further from the track. 'Too much shade makes for ice in winter,' said Gwillym. 'Luenda won't know much about driving in such conditions. I daresay she'll drive the trucks and the Rover round here. We mustn't take it for granted she'll recognise the dangers.'

'We do sometimes have roads closed for ice and snow in the Central Highlands of the North Island,' said Luenda drily. 'It's not all heat and humidity. But I'll be grateful for warnings of what to expect, just the same. And winter will soon be on us judging by those colours.'

Stephen said, 'Gee, we're going to enjoy showing you round, Luenda ... we don't have to keep saying Miss Morgan, do we? We don't often get snow down to lake level, but we've good access to the heights, and our natural swimming-pool in Hazard Valley becomes a skating-rink almost overnight in June, sometimes May.'

'You'll love it,' said Gwillym, 'once you've had your quota of bruises and grazes. Skating's not as easy as it looks. These boys took to it like ducks to water, but you can't expect everyone to take to it as quickly, lads. We'll take it easy with Luenda.'

She was glad the children had run on ahead. Time enough for this dark-browed manager to find out that because you lived in a city, it didn't mean you weren't proficient on the ice. She hid an inward giggle at the thought of her cups. She wouldn't unpack them. Small talk was a great asset, bridging the gap between meeting strangers and becoming acquainted ... they talked of the trip down, the way it lessened the distance, especially when seas lay between, of how a thousand miles means nothing now, and how tired they'd have been coming any other way.

Luenda indicated the brothers. 'Are you two twins or just very near in age?'

Wilkie answered for them. 'Twins, but not identical, praise be, though they're alike. Steve's just that much taller and fairer. If we couldn't tell one from the other there's no knowing what they'd get up to!'

Judith said laughingly, 'Now Di and I have always regretted that we weren't identical. We've missed a lot of fun.'

Wilkie chuckled too. 'Josie Hemmingway's allowing her three boys to come over after our evening meal. They're dying to see you. Nothing like having someone near your own age to make you feel more at home.' She turned to Luenda. 'These poor lambs are entering another world, aren't they?'

Impulsively Luenda said, 'Oh, bless you ... I've been all worked up about bringing three children here, but you understand!'

She wished Gwillym didn't watch her so closely, it made her feel artificial, as if she were acting a part, making up to Wilkie. She'd like to be natural, not have to weigh up every action, every word.

Wilkie said, 'I ought to understand. I once had to do just this myself. My youngest was seven when my husband died. I'd been in shop work when I was single and didn't feel it would be suitable to go back. Shop hours are longer than office hours, and anyway, I wanted to be at home for them after school. So I took a position housekeeping for two bachelors, both getting on, in the Te Anau district, near the lake, but with a road coming to the door, and a school bus stopping at the gate. Frankly I was terrified—entirely without grounds, as it turned out. Those two men were just marvellous with the children. They'd never had a thing to do with young fry before, and even their pranks delighted them. They were born fathers. So no need to get het up, Luenda. I'm not carrying on with Miss Morgan, you'll notice. The children will be fine. I'll check them when they get above themselves, if you aren't around, and do the occasional bit of spoiling all children need, and I'll see to it that *these* crusty old bachelors on Serenity adapt themselves. Even at this age they can get set in their ways. It'll do them good to have three more lively children stirring things up.'

Luenda said, laughing, 'If that's what you want, you've got it!'

Wayne dropped back and relieved Luenda of a bulging shoulder-bag. 'I'm sure that's getting heavier as the ground rises. Let me warn you, Luenda, that dirty crack about our bachelor status is because Wilkie here is a born matchmaker. She's only got to get her eye on any poor fellow still single and she casts about for what *she* thinks is his ideal girl.'

She laughed. 'Forewarned is forearmed! But maybe Wilkie wouldn't regard a girl with the responsibility of three children as ideal.'

Wayne ran an eye over her and he pursed up his lips as if considering it. 'Waal,' he drawled, 'it seems to me your only drawback . . .'

'Could be I look on them as a safety-curtain. Not everyone wants to get married, you know. I say, Mrs Wilkins, is it all right, those children racing ahead?'

'Of course. They're like cats coming to a new place. They want to sniff round, find out the lie of the land, what their new pad is going to offer. Let them be. I told them where they'd find their rooms. But we'll have that tea before you see yours. You ought to be feeling all in.'

The garden's charm lay more in its wildness than in formality, but though weeds were well in evidence, the prodigality of leaf and bloom more than made up for it. Late roses still bloomed on some bushes above pansies and marigolds, asters starred the weedy beds, zinnias looked like circles of embroidery on their stiff stems, and nasturtiums, when they'd run riot everywhere on the ground, had climbed the trees and festooned them with a glorious mixter-maxter of colour.

Wilkie waved a hand. 'The garden went haywire while I was down with the shingles and Gwill was in California. It made the others so busy, there was no time to spare for flowers.'

'I'd love to help, if you can bear anyone else messing about,' offered Luenda. 'It would be heavenly to be able to garden on days other than weekends. You've only got to have three wet Saturdays in a row to lose the battle with weeds.'

'I'd welcome help,' said Wilkie. 'Megan was a born gardener, and one this size takes two people. The boys keep the vegie garden going. You'll see the house fully in a moment.'

It was built of the stone of the surrounding foothills mainly, with deep windowsills and doorways leading off the flagged verandah. What views they would have from here! It was partially glassed-in and well used, she could see, with shabby easy chairs and cane tables, magazine racks and pot-plants. Most of the windows were old-fashioned sash ones, but glass ranch-sliders had been inserted to let more light in and make easy access inside. The front door stood hospitably open and a dark stairway, carpeted in outdated Persian pattern in reds, blues and greens, rose from halfway down the hall.

The children could be heard racing about upstairs. Luenda followed Mrs Wilkins into a long kitchen at the rear of the house, mostly in black and white, from the vinyl on the floor to the tiles at the back of the coal-range that purred cosily at one end, but the curtains were sunshiny yellow and at the other end a fireplace of magnificently coloured stones from the Shotover River had a big log burning. The split stones were all shades from grey to green, and palest pink to lavender, and some of them glittered with mica.

Luenda felt all her apprehensions lifting. She had the strangest feeling that she'd seen this room before. She gazed, puzzled, then she remembered. 'Oh, Mrs Wilkins, there's a strong resemblance in the length of this room, and the two fireplaces, to a faded old picture my grandfather had of *his* grandmother's kitchen in their farm in Wales. I——' to her embarrassment her eyes filled.

She sniffed, wiped her fingertips across her lashes, said, 'Oh, take no notice of me. It's so silly. Only I didn't think I'd find anything here that was dear and familiar . . . and I have.'

Mirabel Wilkins turned to the kettle to let the girl get control of herself without eyes watching, began rinsing a huge teapot and said, 'Luenda, I'm so glad for you. We all need a little bit of our old life to carry over into our new one. I know that for sure.' She added, 'Don't be embarrassed by a bit of honest emotion.'

Luenda smiled mistily, mopped at her eyes and said, 'Thank you. You do understand.' She swung round and encountered Gwillym's gaze. He was standing bulkily in the doorway filling it. She couldn't read his look. Perhaps he doubted she *had* honest feelings.

The twins erupted into the room, Gwillym stepping smartly aside as he heard them coming. 'Luenda, our room is beaut—it's a twin dormer one, with a sloping ceiling and window-seats. That means we can each have one, and bookcases and drawers galore. And a table each, with a drawer in it, we can use as desks.'

Judith cut in, 'And boxes of paints and pastels, and there are already posters pinned up so we won't have to hold back like you said, because of making holes in wallpaper. And we can see the lake and the stables!'

They heard Davy coming more slowly ... not his normal pace ... then suddenly there was a crash and a bang and a tumbling. They all rushed into the hall to see him coming down tucked into a ball, his usual method of falling downstairs, Luenda told them later, a ball that unrolled itself, unperturbed, at the bottom and became a small boy clutching some treasure to his middle, a cylindrical something.

'It didn't break!' he announced triumphantly. 'Gosh, I got a scare ... Luenda, this is the most wonderful thing I ever saw ... it was in my room. It's a long tube with sort of glass at the end and when you shake it it rattles and there must be bits and pieces of coloured glass or something in it, but when you look at it against the light, it forms into sort of carpet patterns, like stained-glass. You've never seen anything like it! What can it be?'

She said, laughing, 'A kaleidoscope. I wonder why we never got you one. Oh, Davy, did you have it to your eye coming down?'

'Yep. Whose is it? How can they bear to give it away? A card against it said, "For David." What do you know about that, Sis?'

Wilkie said, 'It's Gwill's. He thought you might like it.'

Davy beamed. 'That was big of you, Gwill, I bet you know what it is that ... I mean the science of it that makes it go into those patterns.'

The craggy features softened, the eyes crinkled. 'I

ought to be ashamed that I don't know, Davy, but as a matter of fact I——'

Davy prompted him . . . 'Go on—you?'

Gwill looked a little sheepish. 'Sounds daft. I didn't want to know. Some Clever Dick was going to tell me once and I shut him up. I felt it would take away the magic.'

Wilkie nodded. 'And rightly so. I think we can over-explain things. It's good to be able to still wonder at something. Now, after that profound statement, let's get this cup of tea. There's orange drink for the children. Just a wee nibble, mind, because I want you to eat your dinner.'

'No chance of us not doing that,' said Di, 'I'm ravenous!'

Luenda said. 'It's only fair to tell you that Di is always ravenous. The only wonder is where she puts it. Must be super-energy running the calories off.'

'That suits me,' said Wilkie.

When the evening meal, a delicious one, was over, Wilkie surprised Luenda by saying, 'And now, while I scrape the dishes and put them in the dishwasher, Gwill can show you your room, the schoolroom, and the rest of the house.'

So . . . Gwillym was now regarded as the master of Serenity. The host. It was a fascinating house, with the upper floor, like the lower, having little passages running off the big one, where bits had been added to accommodate the big families they had in those days.

Luenda forgot to be stiff and cool with this man who resented her presence here. She made a gesture that embraced them all. 'I feel that every nook and cranny has a history of its own. I'd have loved to have known all these people, from the very first Richards here. I wonder what the first baby to occupy that little room off the master bedroom, under the eaves, was called, and who owned that doll's cradle that swings. And a host of other things.'

'The baby was Llewellyn Rhys Richards—quite a name to encumber a little baby with, but I guess they called him Lew. Were you ever called Lu?'

She shook her head. 'No, my mother liked full names, though she gave in about Davy because the twins found it easier. But my own father used to call me Lindy-Lu. He died when I was seven, but I have such vivid memories of him, and that was what he called me in his most tender moments. Especially at bedtime when he told me my stories.' She was surprised at herself telling this man anything so intimate. This house must be making her nostalgic.

To her equal surprise he said, with a matching nostalgia, 'I envy you that. I haven't even one memory of my father. He died before I was a year old. I've only photographs of him.' He went on rather quickly, 'And Llewellyn's daughter Bronwen owned the cradle. The twins are quite fascinated with it. Llewellyn's father was the first Evan here. He did all this carving. If you feel the frames he did are too heavy, you can take them down from the walls in your room if you wish. He probably had time on his hands when they were so isolated. But they're not everyone's taste.'

'I wouldn't dream of taking them down,' said Luenda. 'It would seem like sacrilege, as if the Richards family was wiped out from memory. I love my room. It's got character—not like any room I ever had before. I like things with a story to them. I just love that converted wash-stand and the white cotton knitted quilt and the little davenport. I'll love writing my letters there. Well, thanks, now I'd better see the schoolroom. I can't let much time go before getting the children into their routine again.'

He shook his head. 'Oh, make it the day after tomorrow. I told them they could have tomorrow off. I think it's necessary for them to get really acquainted with the territory right away. They'll settle better once they've explored.'

She didn't answer promptly, but had to turn away to look at a view from a tiny arched window set into the side of the balcony door of the master bedroom. That gave her time to hold back her protest. *He'd* given the day off to the children. *He* thought they'd settle better that way. Was this to underline that *he* ran things here, even the school hours, as if he indeed owned the lot, and they were here only on sufferance? Would it mean that at times he'd think nothing of interrupting the lesson hours, with requests for help with drafting, lambing, tailing?

For the children's sakes, however, she must not make an issue of it . . . yet! Time enough to assert herself.

Below them they could hear the voices of the three children playing with the Hemmingway boys. Then they heard them greet someone else. Gwill looked out of the window. 'It's Wayne. I guess he's looking for an excuse to come back.'

Luenda didn't answer, but busied herself examining photographs. Wayne called up, 'Some of your letters got into our batch. I think we sorted it too quickly. We found Luenda too distracting!'

Gwill grunted a reply and came back to her. 'Novelty's the thing,' said Luenda softly. 'It'll soon wear off.'

As they left the room he said, 'Not with Wayne. It's a wonder we've kept him as long as this. On some of the farms across the lake, he could be out every night. But he goes off to Ludwigtown and Queenstown for a long weekend once a fortnight on the tourist launch, so he ought to get enough female company then, and does. Don't encourage him.'

She didn't reply.

Wayne was standing by the kitchen table. 'One for you, Gwill, one for Luenda, two for Wilkie.' He looked at one and said, with a sort of fearless effrontery, 'From Sydney, boss. Looks as if our Fenella never gives up.'

Strangely, Gwillym didn't seem to resent it. 'She will. If you don't answer they eventually give up trying.'

It sounded cold, unfeeling, experienced. Luenda looked down on hers quickly, to hide her contempt, then said, 'Oh, this was quick.' The envelope had big blue printing on it. *Daryl Mack Enterprises.* The effrontery seemed to be catching. Gwillym Vaughan said, 'Daryl? The one you shed when you left Auckland?'

There was a moment when a scathing comment about manners trembled on Luenda's lips, then she managed to say coolly, 'You could put it that way. I wanted to start a new existence uncluttered by the past.'

Wayne's reaction was typical. 'Good for you ... and for us. That leaves the field clear!'

'And it's to stay clear. Quite uncluttered. In the last year or two I've had enough emotion to last me a decade.' A very ambiguous statement, had she only known it.

Luenda was tearing her envelope. Gwillym said, 'Perhaps this Daryl has other ideas. Maybe he doesn't intend to stay out of your life. Poor man, everything's against him. Even if he comes a thousand miles, he's still got leagues of water between him and his inamorata.'

There was quite an edge to Luenda's voice. 'I can only think you've got a quaint imagination, Gwillym Vaughan. And really——'

Gwillym's eyes were alight with laughter, which made her crosser than ever. 'And really,' he finished for her, 'it's no business of mine.'

Wayne roared. 'Neither it is. I've been called a cheeky devil tonight, but I reckon I've not got half the cheek you have!'

'And you could be right there,' said Luenda. 'I've never had anyone take an interest in my mail before.'

Gwill said, with suspicious humility, 'But here, on the edge of nowhere, we have to have something to fill up the days.'

Luenda thought she'd better treat it lightly too, and said, 'Well, sorry to disappoint you, but you'll get no vicarious thrills out of my correspondence ... better stick to reading novels!'

She stood at her window that night for a long time. Mount Serenity was veiled in the light of a new moon, silvery rather than golden, a gossamer cloud clinging faintly below its classical peak, just discernible. Yet the rest of the landscape was clear, so that the snows of other mountains shimmered in reflections in the waters of the lake that seemed to stretch out in chilling immensity. No street lights spoke of friendliness, no hum of traffic purred by, on the familiar roads of Mission Bay. Most of all she missed the myriad lights of homes and highways on the score of little hills that made up the mass of Auckland.

A wave of homesickness rose up and engulfed her. A sheep coughed from the nearest paddock, an eerie morepork cry came from the hedge where the little owl must be hunting, and far back along the hills there came a booming note of utter desolation. From her bush-tramping days she recognised it for a bittern, but it was all alien and weird to her that night. When last she had heard that cry, she'd been camped out under the stars with her loved and loving stepfather . . . who had, in his own desolation, brought them to this.

A tide of bitterness, the bitterness she'd refused to allow herself till now, rose up to swamp her . . . how could Dad have done this? She snatched at some form of comfort . . . at least the children didn't know they weren't welcome here. Only she knew that. Knew that across the Tasman a lovely girl was eating her heart out for Gwillym Vaughan, whose real love, within himself, was for land and more land. It looked as if he would stop at nothing to acquire all of the estate for himself. Was it possible that at the end of twelve months, she might find she owned half of it? If she did, then Gwillym didn't know, but would find out, that he had no hope of gaining it by marriage. What a shock he would get when he found out that if indeed the other half was Luenda's, it was forever out of his reach. Suddenly she pulled the blind down on that lovely world outside of shadow and starlight, moon and lake. Its beauty meant nothing to her. And Gwillym Vaughan less than nothing. What was that snatch of verse she'd read recently?

> 'No one can follow me into the midnight,
>   Into the valleys and silence of sleep,

No one can watch me and wonder what ails me,
No one can hear me if, sometimes, I weep.'

Through all the agony of being called to Nevada to
bring home her stepfather's ashes to lie beside her
mother, through all the distressing days when she had
had to comfort the children, reassure them, see to a
thousand and one details of business, to adjust herself
to the numbing shock of finding their security had
vanished and she had an austerity future to face,
Luenda hadn't been able to cry. That release had been
denied her.

But tonight the floodgates were opened. Luenda
wept, and, presently, slept.

They woke to a tang of frost and the air was completely
unadulterated with traffic fumes or factory wastes.
They all came down in trews, with knitted tops pulled
over their shirts. Luenda's short streaky hair was
brushed back from her ears, her fringe slanted across
those darker brows. Her trews were brown and white
checks, the sweater a thick oatmeal one, a green and
brown scarf knotted at her throat. She'd supervised the
children's face-washing when she'd heard Diana say, 'I
reckon we could skip the bathroom this morning—it'd
save time. There's so much to see.' She had brushed
three heads of hair till they shone, and was glad they
scampered ahead of her so eagerly, ready to start their
day.

Wilkie had bowls of porridge ready for them on a
blue-checked cloth, grapefruit juice, eggs, toast. Gwillym
came in two minutes later, freshly-shaved, dark hair still
damp from showering, in a huge fawn cable-stitch
pullover and obviously working trousers.

'Davy can clear the table,' he announced, 'the girls
can make their beds and his, then I'm taking you out in
the Land Rover. It'll be rocky, but we'll leave the
roughest and steepest till you've learned to ride, but
you'll see a good deal of the area from where we'll go.
Tomorrow you'll have your noses to the grindstone, so

make the best of today. Wilkie, we'll be back for lunch, then out again. Windcheaters for all of you—some parts are exposed. You're Aucklanders and we don't want you going down with chills.'

The children, all eagerness, flew off. Wilkie said to Davy, 'Bring those scraps out here to the dogs' bucket.'

Luenda swung round to face Gwillym. 'Must you rub it in at every turn that we're greenhorns? We do know enough to realise when it's cold, you know, to come in out of the rain! You make us feel about as popular as the Danes when they invaded England. This situation was thrust upon us and we're prepared to be adaptable. Evidently you aren't. We may have lived in New Zealand's biggest city, in its hottest city, but that doesn't mean we aren't outdoor types. We lived on the harbour, summer and winter. We were taught to be self-reliant, in fact, with Dad's passion for tramping, even to be toughies. I don't want those children to feel an inferior breed.'

To her surprise and indignation, Gwillym laughed. 'Oh, who'd have thought, when I first saw that elegant model swanning it towards me, that she'd be a spitfire?' The narrow eyes danced. 'And I always did like a spitfire. I can see that our hitherto placid existence here is going to be most interesting from now on.'

She said coldly, 'I'm not in the least interested in your taste in women. For the time being we're partners. But because that means I have to live here this year it doesn't mean I'll put up with the children being made to feel second-rate citizens merely because they're townies. People who were born and brought up in the country can, I suppose, think it confers some degree of strength of character on them. Yet birth and upbringing are very much a matter of luck.' She stopped, said, 'And what are you laughing at now?'

He controlled himself. 'I couldn't help it, my dear Luenda. *I* was born and brought up in the city. Then when I was in my teens my mother married again, Evan Richards's manager. We came here to live in the house the Hemmingways have now. It was an entirely new world to me, straight from a city college to this.'

She had to ask it. 'What city was it?' But she had a horrid premonition about it.

'Auckland,' said Gwillym Vaughan.

For one chagrined moment she glared at him, then her sense of humour rose up to eclipse her humiliation, her gamin grin spread over her face. 'I could choke you for that perfect answer!' she exclaimed and the next moment was laughing with him.

Wilkie and Davy appeared at one door, the girls at the other. 'Can we share the joke?'

'You cannot,' said Gwillym firmly. 'I've just scored over my new partner and I've got such a lovely nature, I won't slap her down further. But she can laugh at herself, so she may suit Mount Serenity down to the ground. You need a sense of humour here.'

'You certainly do,' said Luenda with fervour.

Wilkie beamed. 'This is better. You're not being all stiff and starchy with each other this morning. You'll shake down into one big family yet, which I'm sure was what my dear Megan wanted.'

Like a flash Luenda's uneasiness returned. One family? That could mean two things . . . harmony in living together, or a closer tie. Did Wilkie mean she was sure Megan would have wanted that, or that she *knew* she had?

It could be that when Megan had reached California and settled down for her long holiday there, she had written to Wilkie after meeting Luenda and outlined her wishes. Neither of them had liked Fenella, and Megan, swayed by the long-ago kindness of Luenda's grandparents, had taken an instant liking to her. Their feeling for Fenella had, in fact, gone beyond mere dislike, it had amounted to detestation. Luenda had no time for manipulation of other people's lives. That sort of thing wasn't fair. And if Megan had hinted to Wilkie what she wished, might she not also have hinted to Gwillym? Might that be why he suspected she could, later, inherit the half of the estate she was only to draw the income from meantime?

She didn't know, but she was pretty sure Megan had contrived to get her here mainly on Gwillym's account. Just as well she knew. What a hope!

CHAPTER FIVE

To the children's delight they headed up the valley where it narrowed behind the homestead. It was much steeper than they'd imagined because once they were out of sight of the house, it snaked up in a stiff gradient, while the tumbling stream that had fashioned the valley dropped well below them on its way to the lake.

'Do we have to cross that stream to get to other parts, Gwill?' asked Davy.

'Not this morning. We turn away through the Cleft, a very providential gap, split by nature in the long ago, over to the left, then it widens out to the right, on a sort of plateau through which the stream just meanders. We think that long ago there was a natural rock bridge over it on the plateau, but it had crumbled away, probably in some gigantic flood ... oh, not to be worried, it happened in prehistoric days, and this levelled out evidently, because now there's no danger of water banking up.

'The first pioneers, to gain access to the grazing on the far side, used to have to swim their sheep over, when they put them on the summer basins, which would be a big hurdle, and time-taking, but just before the first Evan died he had a bridge built, and it still survives, well strengthened by modern engineers, though. But it was well constructed in the first place, using the massive rocks from the natural bridge as approaches. They had only to improve on nature. Remember all this,' Gwillym added, 'for I've an idea that one of your first projects for the Correspondence Schools will be to describe your surroundings here. We're nearly to the Cleft ... it's dark and shadowy, isn't it, but we'll be into sunlight shortly.'

The road narrowed, still climbing, but the Land

Rover was powerful and he was an expert driver. They crested the summit, marvelling at the heights which still towered above their wheels, and were into the sunlit plateau, looking east. On a wide strip of turf and tussock, he stopped. 'Pile out and get the view!' He said it exultantly, and with reason.

As far as the eye could see the lake shimmered, truly the Lake of the Kingfisher. Headland after headland, bay after bay reached from the westward ranges at the back of them, and north and south. A dusty-looking track skirted the lake-line eastwards.

Judith said in awed tones, 'Is that track leading to Strathdearn, the nearest station to ours?'

He didn't seem to mind the possessiveness. 'Yes, the bridle-track, something that saved lives in the old days, when help was needed for accident or illness ... or premature birth. It's different now, with good communications. You can see why you should all learn to ride—it can give you a chance to visit other than by launch. Though by boat you save time. You'll all know a lot about boating, coming from Mission Bay. I hope you know about water-safety. This lake is snow-fed, different from being tipped into the Waitemata Harbour and fished out. No one ever goes out on the lake alone, understand? Because though you know the moods of the sea, lake navigation is different. It looks safer, but sometimes the winds can seem to blow from the four points of the compass at once and whip it up like a cauldron.'

Diana moved near him and with a most appealing and spontaneous gesture slipped her hand into his calloused palm. 'You're a good guy, Gwillym, and we won't let you down. You're like our dad—make the rules and expect us to obey them. We were all walloped when we were young for fooling in boats, so we don't.'

Luenda felt a rush of thankfulness. That was how she wanted the children to remember their father, as a strong character, not as the man who'd played ducks and drakes with their security.

They only knew he'd overspent on travelling in an

endeavour to cope with grief. She had been right, then, to preserve that image.

She had to hand Gwillym full marks for his response to that natural gesture. He put his arm round Diana's shoulders when she took her hand out of his, gave her a brotherly hug, said, 'Well, I'll take up where he left off. That eases my mind a lot. This is still largely untamed country and it brings its responsibilities. Look, see that hill with a stand of gums on it, way over . . . that's Strathdearn. You can't see the homestead for trees, but if you look through the binoculars, you can see the station roads above it. That belongs to the MacQueens and the MacGilpins. Rod MacGilpin is married to Emilie MacQueen. It's a partnership.'

Luenda said, 'MacQueen? Where have I heard that name? Oh, of course, but not in farming. That's the name of a big drapery firm in Christchurch. There was a conference of retail drapers in Auckland and my employer wanted me with him to make notes. Old Gaspard MacQueen was a fascinating man, part Scots, part French.'

'It's the same family. Old Gaspard spends half his time at Strathdearn. He made a great success of the drapery . . . inherited it from his uncle, but his heart was in the land. One of his grandsons runs the farm, the other the drapery store. This one married a girl from Southampton.'

The children had moved away, running to the top of the rise to see the lake below. Luenda said, 'Southampton? That's even more drastic than from Auckland to the back of nowhere! How did she take to it?'

Gwillym had a strange note in his voice. What it meant she didn't know. As if he'd only just thought of it that way. 'She loves it here so much she can't tear herself away. Rosamond is a top-notcher. You'd think she'd been an over-lake dweller all her life. She didn't want to stay in Ludwigtown waiting the birth of her little daughter and in the end she nearly scared seven bells out of her husband. He rushed her across lake in his launch, riding it like a speedboat to get her there in time. Oh yes, they made it, but when Rosamond wanted to call her Serena after the mountain, Matthieu refused, said there was nothing whatever serene about her arrival.'

Luenda chuckled too. To her own surprise she found herself saying indignantly, 'Well, anyway, Mount Serenity is on *this* station. That name should be reserved for a baby born here.'

She looked up and encountered a strange look in the enigmatic eyes she'd thought were dark brown at first, only to find them green, with tawny flecks. He said quickly, 'You *have* identified with the place, haven't you?'

A hot flush spread from her throat. 'You didn't correct Judith, or set her back in any way, when she said "ours". I see *I'll* have to watch every word I say, and I'm not good at it.'

He said gently, 'Don't be so touchy, Luenda. I didn't say I didn't like it. I know I was hostile when I first heard what Megan had done. The first shock of finding myself——' he stopped.

Her tone had a hint of bitterness. 'Of finding yourself saddled with a greenhorn and having to share a property like this for a whole year.'

He pulled her round to face him. 'That's more blunt than I'd have put it.' He seemed at a loss, then, 'Let's just say I'm far from hostile now. There could be ... compensations.'

Warning bells rang for her. She found the touch of his hands upon her arms—right through her jersey, disturbing. She felt impatient with herself. That could be exactly what he wanted. 'Compensations for you, perhaps, not for me.'

The fingers bit in. His eyes narrowed. 'What do you mean? Of course there are compensations for you ... all with the dollar sign on them.'

Her face whitened. 'That's a caddish thing to say! I——' she choked.

To her immense surprise he said immediately, 'I'm

sorry. It *was* a caddish thing to say. I apologise. I can't think what possessed me to say it, except that you made me mad.'

'Well, that makes two of us,' she said shortly. 'I don't understand your reactions to having us here. The only reason for such resentment must also have the dollar sign on it. But even if Megan hadn't made this magnificent gesture to us, it's not to say everything would have come to you. It could have gone to Gillian, even if it seems she doesn't need it. You could have still been managing that half for an absentee owner in the States. But I think Gillian must have made it plain that enough had been provided for her and her family earlier and she might have been quite happy for her sister to do this for me. In fact——' she stopped abruptly, she'd nearly said she *knew* Gillian would have liked the idea. It had been in her time of greatest need that Grandfather had come to her aid.

Gwillym didn't ask her to continue. 'I know. When Megan was dying, they called me, so I spent some time with the family.' He looked a little bleak. 'I didn't get there in time. I was, after all, like the grandson she never had. Hers and Evan's.' His lips tightened, lines grooved themselves more deeply each side of his mouth. 'And let me tell you, Luenda Morgan, it wasn't because of the estate. There was a very real bond between Megan and Evan and myself from the moment I arrived up on school holidays to work here, when my mother became engaged to my stepfather, their manager. The next year they were married and I was offered a job up here. My sisters were working in Auckland, Mum and Dad were newlyweds, and I could have felt very out of it if it hadn't been for Megan and Evan. They took me to live here at first, to get used to things. I was the odd man out till then. We owe it to Megan that it developed into a very healthy relationship. I'd never had a father and had to get used to it. He's a grand fellow who was very patient with an awkward and resentful teenager. But most of it was due to Megan Richards. When Mum and Dad retired in Dunedin, she offered me the job as

manager. I never looked for any benefits to come. I did
hope to buy in to the estate in time, and that's——'

He got no further. 'This time *I'm* sorry. I'd not
realised quite what the situation was. Look,' she added,
'we've been thrust into this sort of working partnership.
I don't even know what's at the end of this year. I don't
know how the children will settle when the novelty's
worn off. At present it's like a holiday to them. I
haven't even got to grips with the financial side of it
and I don't dare ask ... after a dirty slam about my
compensations for being here all having the dollar sign
on them. But not knowing doesn't exactly make one
feel secure, and feeling insecure can make anyone ...
prickly!'

His grip stopped hurting, though he still held her.
The hawklike face gentled a little. 'I should have told
you. We're to see the Queenstown solicitor shortly. I
thought it best the children should settle to schoolroom
routine a few days first before having a day off over
there. I draw a monthly salary. The cheques for wool
and lamb and cattle sales go into the general account,
of course. It's all done by our accountants. You'll draw
a salary too, and there's a good allowance for the
children. I would have made this quite plain to you
earlier ... when we first met ... only I thought——'

'Go on ... you thought what?'

He pulled a rueful face. 'The last few seconds we
seem to have come to a more amicable understanding
of each other and I didn't want to set you off again.
Don't look like that, I don't mean you're liable to go
off half-cocked, I just mean that this is a tricky
situation and I'd rather we didn't get at cross-purposes.'

'Fairly spoken. Go ahead.'

'I didn't think you could possibly feel insecure with
all your assets. You'd sold a launch and a dinghy, two
cars, even before I met you. And the house since. I still
think that was hasty, because we don't know what will
happen eventually. You'd have been better to have let
the house. But you've burned your boats. I've an idea
your solicitor will have advised you to invest the money

you got and draw on it for immediate expenses, so I thought this could wait. Houses in Auckland bring fantastic prices.'

It seemed a tight band was restricting Luenda's heart. It was no good. She couldn't bear to see contempt for her stepfather flash into these eyes. She said, 'There wasn't as much as we'd thought. I wanted the balance of what was over when a mortgage was repaid to remain intact for the children's later lives.' The next words almost stuck in her throat. 'I'll take the salary from the estate, though you can hardly call it that, I suppose. My main task will be supervising lessons for my brother and sisters. But I promise you this—I'll pull my weight in the house chores and farm chores as much as I've time for.'

There! He could think she was after all she could get out of the estate.

He said slowly, 'I doubt if you could stand up to many of the farm chores. After all, it's a bit different, from modelling clothes to picking up dirty tail-end wool. That's about all we could use you on. Women students tackle it sometimes, so I suppose you could.'

Suddenly she stamped her foot. 'I'm *not* a model! You've got your lines crossed. You've got to stop thinking of me as one. I *told* you—that it was only in an emergency. Zena, the top model, sprained her ankle falling about a miserable six inches off the dressing-stand. I was press-ganged into that. I was the only one with the approximate measurements and almost the same colouring. In fact there was a bit more of me than of Zena, so that made it worse.'

'What do you mean . . . worse?'

'You know! Don't tell me you don't know. There was hardly any top to that dress. I couldn't wear a bra with it. I hated every moment of it . . . with that crowd gawking at me . . . you included.

Gwillym said, with a remembering look in his eyes, 'You didn't look as if you hated it.'

The colour of anger stung her cheeks. 'That shows how well I must have carried it off! I'd do anything for my boss. He's been one in a thousand and he was having one hell of a day in any case. Zena spraining her ankle was the last straw. I was Mr Ackroyd's secretary, not a model. Honestly, when I walked out in that dress I knew exactly how Lady Godiva must have felt!'

He flung back his head and gave a great bellow of laughter. She was furious. 'It's all right for you to laugh! *You* didn't have to wear it!'

He tried to sober up but failed. 'No, my dear termagant, and just as well . . . I'm not exactly equipped for it.' He made an appropriate gesture. Luenda continued to glare.

'When I saw that dress I almost refused. But it had been announced and Big Joe was in such a state that day I couldn't upset him further.'

Gwillym looked amazed. 'Was he as worked up as all that about a fashion show?'

'No.' Her tone was withering. 'His daughter was having a baby. She'd had a frightful accident when she was pregnant and was so determined not to miscarry her baby, she was no less than a heroine. But we were all worked up for her. We got the news right after the parade that she'd had a large son, perfect and beautiful. Big Joe was so excited he hugged me and I kissed him. Goodness, when I was a scared junior in that office at eighteen I'd never have imagined getting so carried away!' A moment later she was asking, 'What are you looking like that for?'

He grinned crookedly and looked five years younger. 'This is a new experience for me . . . looks as if I'm going to spend most of my time apologising to you. I rang the solicitor's office when I came off the plane, only to be told he was at North Shore. I asked where you worked as otherwise I mightn't have time to see you, and was sent to Ackroyds. The office said you were modelling. When you came on in that dress I groaned inwardly. I could imagine the sort of harm you'd cause up here among the men on a womanless sheep-station—bar Wilkie and Josie.

'When I thought you'd had time to get out of the

wretched thing I asked for you and was sent back to the office. I was just in time to see you in what looked like a passionate clinch with your boss. He didn't look old enough to be a grandfather, damn it. He wasn't bald, wasn't even grey. I couldn't see his face ... you were too busy kissing it!'

Luenda was laughing helplessly. 'He's the most upright man you could imagine. No knee-patting, no familiarity, and his wife's a darling. Gwillym, we actually stayed the night with them before leaving Auckland! And you needn't worry about me being a *femme fatale* up here. Look, I'm so ordinary. I was a freckle-faced, tow-headed urchin of a child. That heavy make-up for the parade fooled you. It gave you a wrong impression entirely.'

He looked down on her and his lips twitched. 'And yet in your brother's eyes, you knock 'em out like ninepins. Yessir, as Davy informed me when you left him to make small talk to me.'

Luenda gasped, 'You've got to be joking! Davy would think that clunky ... his favourite word for girls' talk. If the girls start raving about some idol of theirs he thinks they're the sloppiest things. He wouldn't say *that*. Oh dear, I'll offend you again, but you *must* have misunderstood!'

He said deliberately, 'I didn't, you know. He even said, "But my sister doesn't know her own charm. She's so keen on going to this lake, she doesn't care that Daryl Mack is breaking his heart." '

Her astonishment was too real to be assumed. Her mouth fell open. Then she said feebly, 'I can't fathom it. What on earth could make *Davy* say a thing like that? Now if it had been the girls I could credit it—they're hopelessly romantic. There isn't a grain of truth in it.'

'Isn't there? A letter from him followed you down so promptly it arrived with us.'

Luenda laughed. 'Not a letter, just a receipt. I thought a cheque of mine had gone astray. It was important and I didn't know what the mail arrangements here were. I asked Daryl, by phone, to check it out, and he thought it might miss me at the house. He was little more than a good friend. We used to partner each other to things. I'm glad it's wound up. People were taking it for granted we'd get engaged some time. I thought it might keep some other girl away from him. I never had an atom of the right feeling for him.'

'It could also have kept other chaps away from you,' Gwillym observed.

'Well, I didn't care if it did. The last two years since Mother first took ill, I've had other things to think about.'

She freed herself from his hands. 'The children will be back in a moment, and they might wonder at this. We got tense, didn't we? As it is they'll probably ask what we laughed so loudly at. For heaven's sake don't mention the Lady Godiva bit. They've no idea I hated wearing that last model. It's as dead as the dodo now.'

He nodded. 'We've cleared the ground, haven't we? No misunderstandings left. No forlorn suitors cluttering your path. Good.'

Good? Then she was right; this man did have intentions.

She ignored it. His motives for thinking it good would bear watching. They too had the dollar sign on them.

Things settled into routine. Josie Hemmingway was a great help to Luenda in organising the work in the schoolroom, so that it suited life on the farm.

'They've got no bus ride or walk to school, so they save that much time, and you can start them earlier than nine. I get them into the schoolroom right after breakfast. They get cracking on things they can manage by themselves till I've got the beds made and the dishes washed. Then I get down to the oral stuff before I have to start preparing lunch. I give them just three-quarters of an hour's break then, so with the early start, school is finished for the day at two, and off they go to play.

They'll be able to have more organised games now your three are here.

'A fairly rigid timetable is the answer, otherwise you get behind, and if we do have a day off across-lake that isn't a Saturday or Sunday, they work till half-past three the other days that week to make up the time. And probably they've not told you that the Ludwig Primary School takes them for a week every term, billeting them out among their children. Marvellous for them. They arrange matches and outings.'

'What a good idea!'

'And when the children get to High School age, they go to the hostel over there from Monday morning till Friday night. It's not too bad. I couldn't stand having them board in Dunedin and seeing them only in the holidays.'

'Of course I don't know if I'll be here longer than a year, but——'

Josie cut in, 'I do hope you are. Even in ten days I feel different. The men are fun, but at times I yearn for woman-talk. Wilkie is a dear and so was Megan, but you're not so far from my own age as they were. I'm sure Megan must have made some pretty good arrangements for next year. I think she wanted you to stay here but felt you ought to have a taste of the isolated life first. Besides, you sold your house, didn't you?'

Luenda hesitated only a moment. She just naturally trusted Josie. She told her the whole story. 'I don't want the children to know. They're too young to be so disillusioned.'

Josie pursed her lips in a soundless whistle. 'You mean . . . you were left to carry the whole can? With the three of them?'

Luenda nodded. 'At first it was horribly frightening. I thought there mightn't be enough to even settle all the debts. But the house fetched more than I'd thought, and after the repayments, it left enough for a small nest-egg towards the children's higher education, but not enough for a deposit on a house, even an old, small one. So this was a godsend. I'm the cuckoo in the nest, of course, as far as Gwill's concerned, but I can't help that. It would have been fitting had the whole thing come directly to him, but beggars can't be choosers, so I sank my pride and accepted half of this year's income. But I couldn't tell him what Dad had done, he'd have thought us all scroungers.'

Josie looked at her sideways, unknown to Luenda. 'I can understand that. These days we women don't like to feel dependent, but ... don't be too proud, Luenda. He's a great guy, and after all, his mother knew what it was to have to work to support her family in the days when there was no equal pay. He'd understand more than you think. It's not as if he's always owned half a sheep-station.'

Josie thought: 'But there's something more personal here. I'd better not say too much.' She waited a moment, then said, 'I know it seems mysterious Megan getting you here for a year before the final settlement of that half, but who knows what she had in mind? I'm sure, even now, you can take this life, but Megan saw you only in your Auckland setting and couldn't have been sure. I'm a great believer in taking a day at a time, letting things work themselves out. I can keep my own counsel. I think it's wise not to let the children know their father gambled their security away. Children see things in black and white. When they're older, if they have to know, they'll have had enough experience of life to realise that grief does strange things to people. Given time your stepfather would have come to himself, taken hold of the situation, retrieved it, probably, but his heart gave out before he could.'

Josie took Luenda's hands in hers. 'Right now you must be missing your friends, your work, your independence, your own home, but you've got what it takes—I know that. And we're delighted with the change in Wilkie. She missed Megan so much, grew listless, uncaring, but with all of you to cook for, she's already looking better, and as for Gwillym ...' she paused.

Luenda looked at her warily, then laughed. 'Come on

now, Josie, be honest! Gwillym is like any man would
be whose home is invaded and whose inheritance is in
jeopardy possibly.'

Josie blinked. 'Is he? Now for some reason he looks
to me like a man who suddenly knows which way he's
going, and he didn't always.'

Luenda shrugged, 'Oh, I think he knows which way
he's going. But I'm not sure if it's what he prefers.'

To herself she added: But he may not find the pot of
gold at the rainbow's end for all that.' She knew now
what she would do. She'd seem to go along with him.
And, at the end, if it so happened some of the estate
came to her, Gwillym Vaughan would find he wasn't
going to acquire it by marriage!

The promised day in Queenstown proved a perfect one
weatherwise. This dry, late autumn weather, with the
nip in the mornings and the brilliant noons, was
glorious, invigorating, sparkling.

Josie and the children went with them, and Wilkie,
who had packed a picnic hamper laden with goodies.
The children all had spending money for toys and
books, and they made an early start across the wide
lake, as the appointment with the solicitor was for ten-
thirty and they had to pick up a hired car from the
garage in Ludwigtown to get them across to
Queenstown.

As they ascended the stairs Gwillym said, 'No
curiosity today, Luenda—it would worry Mr Stillman.
This has been a complicated business for him. I
wouldn't like him to think that in any way I wasn't
happy with Megan's wishes in this matter.'

She didn't know what to make of that, so she just
agreed. Mr Stillman was a sweetie. He quietly appraised
her, Luenda felt, but she also felt he rather liked what
he saw. He said, 'I'd have liked to have talked all this
over with Mrs Richards, but her time was so regrettably
short that she did the best she could with the Los
Angeles solicitor who acquainted me with the whole
situation.

'It's unusual, but she left this sealed letter to be opened when the year is up. Meanwhile, Miss Morgan, the income from half the estate is to be yours this year, and it's quite neatly tied up to provide for the children's needs, clothing, education, pocket-money, even insurances. I've worked it out on a monthly basis, and the stipulation that you live on Serenity for a year is very happily contained within the New Zealand tax year, from April till the end of March next year. It just worked out that way, but much easier than overlapping two tax years. By then you'll know what it's like to live through all four seasons, and the toughest, the winter, you'll get over first.

'There are some documents for your signature. Not much else to be done yet. I've opened an account for you in your name at this bank here, and they want you in today for specimen signatures. You can draw cheques immedately. I thought to safeguard you, this first period, by holding back the approximate amount you'll need to pay in tax in September and March. You'll have been used to pay-as-you-earn tax being deducted from your weekly wage, and switching to the provisional tax framework is tricky at first.' It was all so matter-of-fact, Luenda began to feel less of a usurper.

They came out, and went to the bank. Gwill asked, 'Aren't you drawing anything?' She felt gratified to be able to reply, 'No, I won't need to till we come over again.'

They came out and were heading for the beach where they were to rendezvous with the rest, but Gwillym said, 'Let's have a cup of tea first on our own.'

'Why, couldn't we go straight——'

'Don't you feel the need of some mild celebration after getting all that settled?'

She looked at him sharply. Was that a sly dig at the way this windfall had dropped into her lap?

She made herself say carelessly: 'Well, I'm not exactly in a champagne mood, but yes, a cup of tea.'

With that ordinary small pleasure, sitting down at a

table and being waited upon, things seemed different suddenly. She was a well-dressed girl, with a personable man, having tea for two. He must have felt that too, for he said, 'We need these small touches of civilisation from time to time, you know. It's not all work and no play. It's amazing how much coming and going fills the year. Parties of farmers from the north, with wives, arrive at the station for a field day, even representatives from other countries not far from here, interested in trade—Japanese, Fijians, Australians. There are dances in Ludwigtown. We get invited to tourist promotion affairs, quite glamorous ones, church celebrations ... you'll be surprised how little time you'll get to be lonely.'

Luenda took another sandwich. 'You sound now as if you're trying to sell me the over-lake life. As if you wanted me to stay.'

It was meant to be mocking, but he took it seriously. 'I do,' he said, and the green eyes looked meaningly into hers.

Her lashes flickered, and she said involuntarily, 'You know, when we first met, I thought you had dark eyes. But they're green.'

He looked surprised and grinned. 'What's that to do with anything? Are you trying to head me off?'

She grinned back. 'You'd better get used to that. I embarrass myself sometimes, by uttering the first thing that comes into my head. The girls tease me about it. Mother tried to break me of it. We got a new minister when I was quite small, and instead of greeting him with a hullo, I looked up and said, "Why have you got only one dimple?" '

Gwillym said, cocking an eyebrow at her. 'I'd find that a refreshingly candid change ... you uttering uncensored remarks. You've been very cagey with me, really. Guarded, in fact.'

She said soberly, 'That was natural. I'd never been wished on to anyone before, and I was scared.'

'I'm very happy to have you wished on to me,

Luenda. I wasn't at first, I admit, especially after—no, I won't say that.'

She laughed, 'You were going to say after the shock of seeing me in that daring dress.'

'Yes. I thought you'd be a man-eater, cause havoc up here.' He deliberately moved his foot against hers under the table till she could feel the warmth of his leg against hers. 'But now why wouldn't I want you to stay? Not many men would suddenly acquire a partner as lovely as mine.'

She giggled. 'That's a remnant of that first impression ... the make-up. I told you I'm just a tow-headed freckle-faced type.'

'I like the freckles scattered on that nose. It's a very nice nose, by the way, in the classical style. And your mouth is well cut.' As his eyes lingered on her lips, she was annoyed to feel a blush rising.

His eyes ran over the lime-green elegance of her suit, with a white frilly blouse beneath it. A thin gold chain lay against the smooth brown of her throat, pale green olivine earrings dangled from the tiny lobes of her ears; his gaze lingered on the short hair with the deep swirl.

He said, 'By the way, if you happen to want a shampoo and set one of the hairdressers could probably work you in. They fit in appointments for unexpected visits from the over-lake women.'

'No, thanks. If I want it cut next time I'll have it done, but I'll ring to make sure. I'll wash it myself tomorrow. I've been doing that ever since I arrived. It dries very quickly.'

Gwillym looked surprised. 'But can you put those goldy streaks in yourself? I like them.'

She stared. 'Those streaks don't come out of a bottle, dear man. I've always had them. In summer they get even more bleached on top. I know lots of women do get lights put in, and it's a good idea to highlight your hair, but I don't need to.' She looked saucy. 'Thought me a bit artificial, didn't you? Anything else I need to clear up? You could have quite a few surprises ahead of you in the months to come, finding out things about your partner!'

She'd never seen so warm a look in those green, brown-flecked eyes. 'So I think,' he said, 'and I find I'm looking forward to it.'

Luenda decided to treat it coolly. 'I thought it was women who had the reputation for changing their minds.'

'People who never change their minds are either boring or dangerous. They suffer from stagnation. I ought to have known better than to rely on a first impression. But even in the short time you've been at Serenity, I've come to admire you.'

She dimpled, 'If my legs weren't tucked under this table I'd drop a curtsey and say, "Thank you, kind sir." Sorry not to reciprocate, but as I had no strong feelings about you at first meeting, there's not much room for change. I felt, rather tolerantly, I prided myself, that it was natural you weren't pleased at the way things had been left. I knew you were heated over it. I was tepid, and I've stayed that way. All I want, Gwillym, is a pleasant existence for this year for my sisters and brother. No fireworks. Let's keep it that way, please.'

'Keep it tepid? I don't think Central Otago breeds tepid people. In a year's time you won't even be the same girl, Luenda.'

She shrugged. 'Who cares? Josie told me to take a day at a time, and that's what I'm doing.'

Gwillym was keeping a good rein on himself. No wonder . . . for him there was a lot at stake. He merely chuckled, 'I've never enjoyed sparring verbally with a girl before, but I find I do. I think I'm being paid back for my first reaction to you—and no wonder! You'll get it out of your system that way, Luenda.'

'You're making too much of it. It's not important. Let's get back to the others. My guess is that the children will be starving, and it's not exactly a summer day.'

However, they had found a sheltered spot under the great trees that circled Queenstown Bay and they'd been enchanted with the little black teal that actually stayed under water for a few moments, plainly visible in the pellucid waters, scuttling along the bottom at the shallow edge, hunting for food. And they had watched the jet-boats setting off with the tourists, scarlet-hulled and garlanded with spray.

No one watching would have thought of them as other than a closely-united family group. Then they strolled round the former goldmining town, shopping for all sorts of things, Fergus, Robbie and Duggie displaying adult possessiveness in showing off a new territory to these cityites from the North.

Gwillym showed a new side to Luenda, quite an avuncular one, buying them books and puzzles, icecreams and novelties. Luenda felt more of the ice round her heart begin to thaw. The children were having such a happy, happy day, and it wasn't done with intent either, because Josie said to her quietly, 'He's always like this. My boys just love him. Not cupboard love with them, either; he's very good at showing them things, even when busiest.'

Gwill looked at his watch. 'We'll have afternoon tea across at the cottage in Ludwigtown. Luenda might like to see it.'

That would be where Mirabel Wilkins would retire eventually. Luenda wondered if anything might be said. She hoped the day would be far distant; it would be an awkward domestic situation otherwise.

They came into the little town with the westering sun striking splashes of pure gold from the larches and poplars on the dark hillside over the gorge. On this side the river bank was wide and shingly and almost level, scattered with the beautifully coloured stones of Central. Across the other side of the swift water the cliffs, clothed with bush, rose steeply, and after rain, she was told, the hillsides glittered with waterfalls that lasted only a day or two. On the southern side the town sloped down to the lake. The river wound round the back of the houses and didn't enter the lake for many miles eastward.

There was a magnificent avenue of chestnuts, aspen

poplars all a-quiver, sycamores, golden ash, limes, resplendent in russet and flame, yellow and orange. Each side of them, over a narrow footpath, lilliput houses, obviously built in the gold-rush days, squatted close to the footpaths and to each other, painted now in pastel shades, modernised, and with creepers clinging lovingly to the rough outlines. 'Oh, they're just like dolls' houses!' cried Luenda in enchantment.

Gwillym said, 'They huddled together because when they were built this was a vast untamed land, cruel and relentlessly cold because there were so few trees to break the force of the snow-laden winds. They came up from the South Pole, whistled across the lake from the high-tops, so every bit of shelter was welcome. How they got their first saplings to survive we know not.

'We own one of these, almost the last one at the far end, and the land widens there because the river sweeps back so we have a little orchard and nut trees, a small vegetable garden, swings and a cricket pitch. It means we can come over for a weekend when we like, and not worry if the tourists have swallowed up all the accommodation. Josie sometimes stays here with the boys when they have their week at the primary school. You could too, Luenda. It would give you a break from Serenity.'

She was conscious of a strong, unexpected emotion. She didn't *want* a break from the sheep-station. The consciousness of it hit her bang between the eyes. She said quickly, because it was expected of her, 'That would be wonderful.'

They pulled up at the second last cottage. Its rough walls, hewn from local stone, were whitewashed and the old-fashioned sash window-frames were outlined in pale blue. The roof had been replaced with a modern one, though; no doubt the original had leaked. But it was black decramastic and harmonised. The curtains were in accord with its period, of white Nottingham lace, and the narrow path that led to its scarlet front door was of herringbone brick, with seeding candytuft each side. On one side well back from the house, great pines made a soughing sound, and at the corner of the house, spindleberries were opening coral cases to show orange seeds inside and wax-eyes were perching there, pecking away. 'That tree is to keep the witches away,' said Wilkie.

Gwillym took an enormous key from his pocket, went to fit it in the door, changed his mind and handed it to the housekeeper. 'There you are, Mirabel, it's all yours now.'

She flushed with pleasure. 'It will always belong to Mount Serenity Station and the folk there as far as I'm concerned. It's a family holiday house. It's been a lifeline for so long and at times a refuge. I love it.'

It was bigger than it looked because it had been added to through the years and straggled out at the back in two long wings that made a small sheltered courtyard in between, where old iron footscrapers stood and pots of geraniums could survive under the wide eaves all winter. Fergus went racing through. 'C'mon, Davy, have a look at our bedroom, it's got four bunks so you can sleep there some time. It's got the rumpus-room leading off it, a table-tennis table, model railway 'n' all.'

Wilkie said, 'You girls can go upstairs to see the bedroom you'll have.' They looked mystified, and she laughed. 'Open that cupboard door, it's a secret stair.' Intrigued, they did just that. Wilkie said, 'I'll go up after them. I've some things here for my room—fresh pillowcases and so on.'

Luenda was left with Gwillym. She looked about her. 'I love it. I'm so glad Wilkie has somewhere like this when she gives up at Serenity, her very own. Will she feel lonely?'

He shook his head. 'She has it all mapped out, though I hope it won't be for years yet. It's always a hassle to get children into the hostel. She's planning to take some of the overflow here, especially the over-lake children she knows.' He hesitated. 'So if you do stay on, Luenda, you need have no worries about Judith, Diana and Davy.'

If. But the years beyond this year were still uncharted for her. The silence grew, an awkward silence.

He said, jerkily, 'Come and see the rest of the downstairs apart from this sitting-room.'

An old kitchen with a coal-range, a rag rug, blue willow-pattern china on a scrubbed whitewood dresser. Homely, an air of security. There was a small bedroom off it, and a passage out of which opened two more bedrooms, one so large it must have been two rooms knocked into one. It was all soft fuchsia shades, rosy pink, with purple and lavender. A chintzy room. Gwillym said, 'So many couples have honeymooned here we call it the Bridal Suite.'

'Friends from the cities, no doubt, wanting a country honeymoon.'

He thought, then laughed. 'No, oddly enough most of them have been over-lake couples. As if they couldn't get enough of the Lake of the Kingfisher. Oh, they usually went further afield for the latter part, but they spent their first few nights here.'

Luenda forgot she was tough where this man was concerned. Stars lit her eyes. 'I think that's lovely, to so identify oneself with the place where one lives that the happiest days of all had to be spent beside its shores. Who says the modern age isn't romantic?' She felt an unaccustomed rush of emotion run over her, as if here, in this cottagey room, she'd found something she'd only hoped had existed. She didn't want to analyse that feeling, she was afraid of it, so she said hastily, 'I suppose they'd be married in one of the churches of Ludwigtown?'

He looked down on her with an unreadable expression—not stern. 'Not all. Some were married from the Chapel-on-the-Water. It belongs to Twin Hills Station, and it's the biggest station on the lake. My mother and stepfather were married there. It stands out on a promontory, one of the headlands that shelter their bay. Mother met Dad up there, you know, when she was visiting a friend who was their governess. He'd been at Mount Serenity a long time. He was a lonely

sort of chap till he met Mum, very well liked. It was
something you'd never forget—a perfect summer day in
January.

'It was quite a spectacle to see the minister and the
guests setting out across the water, from all the bays
and from here, coming in to the jetty, tying up, walking
to the headland. There was a huge reception in their old
ballroom, and there was I, thrilled to see my mother the
centre of admiration, looking so beautiful and so
young, but as jealous as heck of the new man in her life!
But Gus was marvellous. He'd handled so many raw
farm cadets he had infinite patience, and he knew it
would take time. He became my hero—still is.'

Luenda looked up at him, brushed her bang sideways
as she always did when moved, and said, 'Thank you
for telling me. I like that.'

A new friendliness sat upon them.

Gwillym looked down on her, smiling, as she looked
up. 'I've always thought,' he said deliberately, 'that I'd
like to be married there myself.'

In a flash, corroding that tender moment with
distrust, Luenda remembered that lovely girl, Fenella
Newbolt, eating her heart out for Gwillym, in
Australia, Fenella who had been the current governess
at Twin Hills. Had she too planned a wedding in the
Chapel-on-the-Water?

The moment of magic had gone.

CHAPTER SIX

LUENDA flung herself into the busy life of the station in a fine endeavour to leave herself no time to examine her own feelings, these strange feelings so unfamiliar to her . . . the traitorous unguarded ones that swept over her when she appreciated Gwillym's ways with the children, with his men, with the animals. Other feelings, physical ones, when he'd touch her hand passing her something, put a comradely arm about her shoulders. When she longed for more than that. Till now she had deemed herself a cold fish, had been a stranger to desire. Work, that was the answer.

She and Wilkie got into the neglected garden, raking up leaves into huge bonfires, where the six children roasted potatoes in the ashes for after-school snacks, and demolished weeds and dug over the beds in great haste before the winter frosts made them too hard. The chrysanthemums that had lit every corner with bronze and white, yellow and clover rosettes, were gathered and brought in to continue their lighting-up in the huge urns and vases of the old house, carefully tended by removing leaves higher and higher so they would last as long as possible.

Wilkie was preserving leaves and berries and drying heads of hydrangeas which up here turned into lovely metallic colours, copper, verdigris green, dull blue. They gathered bulrushes from the edge of the lake, yarrow heads from the track verges, and snow-grass and tussock from the heights, for Wilkie to make exquisite artistic arrangements with her collection of driftwood, bleached and planed by countless decades of waters into shapes of sheer beauty. Luenda liked to watch Gwillym polishing and shaping some of them for her.

Sometimes Wilkie insisted they take a break. 'It's over the hills and far away for us today,' she'd say.

'Might as well while this glorious dry sunshine lasts. There are umpteen bays in this property they haven't seen yet and they're doing that project on the tussock varieties of the high-country, so they can gather specimens as they go. You work far too hard, Luenda. You more than earn your keep, you know. The way you help me keep the tins full, and stock the deep-freeze up, has made all the difference to me.'

Luenda said seriously, 'So I should. We're four extra—quite an addition to any household, especially the way we live here. Our table at home was never frugal, even the last year or two, but this is positively lavish.'

'It tends to be that way on farms, there's so much meat and produce available. And all those eggs! Judith is making a reputation for herself with those fowls. She's got their quarters so comfy they're actually roosting in there at nights now. She feeds them last thing in there, of course, and they follow her with such devotion. Cupboard love, I suppose.'

A voice spoke behind them. 'It's not all cupboard love,' said Gwillym. 'Even when she hasn't wheat or mash in her hands, they follow her with adoration, and the bantams all squat down to be stroked. And that rooster used to be so savage, but now, blow me down, he follows Judith like a lamb, even to trotting behind when Steve's giving Judith her riding lesson.'

Luenda burst out laughing. 'I know. It looks so funny. Steve said to me yesterday it's as well Dobby's so quiet. The wretched bird's jealous! Di's finished her lessons. She's a natural with horses, of course. I'm thrilled about it. That's one thing I've been glad of, because the riding-schools up north were so expensive.'

Wilkie had disappeared. Gwillym's brows came down. '*One* thing? Only one?'

Luenda flushed. 'Sorry, that didn't sound very gracious ... or grateful.' Then because she couldn't help it, she added, 'Most of the other things I'm glad about are financial things. Like you said, all with the dollar sign on.'

To her surprise, because that tanned, weatherbeaten skin didn't show colour easily, he reddened too. Then he looked her straight in the eye and said, 'I'm ashamed of that. It ought never to have been said. I've watched the way you don't waste things. There's plenty and to spare in a self-supporting station like this, but household expenses can still get out of hand. Somebody brought you up well. It's good to meet up with thrift in a modern girl.'

She said slowly, 'Till Mother married again, she had to be very careful with the bawbees.' Nothing about that last horrible time when she had to be so cheeseparing, denying the children so much she longed to give them, pretending it was just till things were settled.

A silence fell. Gwillym said after a moment or two, 'We've cancelled out my remark about the dollar signs. We'll cancel out yours too about there being financial compensations. So I'll ask my question again. Don't you find any other things to recompense?'

Luenda scooped up some scattered leaves off the newspapers spread on the kitchen table, keeping her head bent. 'I do. Many.'

'Such as?'

She made an impatient gesture. 'You're always so persistent, Gwill. Do you want them itemised? Does it matter?'

'Would I ask if it didn't? If it didn't matter?'

She looked up at him, searchingly. 'I don't know. Often I don't understand what you're getting at, Gwillym.'

The green eyes danced. 'You don't have to. Isn't it rather intriguing not to understand people fully? I don't understand you. I never have ... and I find that intriguing too.'

She shrugged, said lightly, 'You've lost me. Like I said, you're an enigma to me.'

He let that go. 'What other things compensate. Luenda-spelt-with-one-L? If ever you have a daughter named after you, I think you should make it the proper

Welsh way and add another L at the beginning and an H at the end. Come on, what other things?'

She said coolly, 'I like the unpolluted air. I like Mount Serenity in all its moods. I like looking out of my windows at sunset or sunrise and thinking as far as I can see I have the right to wander. It's not mine, but I'm here and have the freedom of the station. I like to drift off to sleep to the sound of lake-waters lapping at the shore. I'm overwhelmingly grateful to God that the children haven't been homesick. It could be that leaving all that was dear and familiar to them was only a little sorrow compared to losing Mother and Dad. They love it here.'

Gwillym said, 'Then you must consider staying when the year ends.'

She ignored that. He was only saying it because he feared that when the year ended she might inherit the half of it. She went on, 'I love the way the other station women ring up and chat to me, even if till now they didn't want to expose their children to the risk of chickenpox. Wilkie forbade them to come, which was pretty unselfish of her. They're coming soon now. I love Wilkie, she makes me feel loved and secure.'

'Hm, I was wondering when something more personal would crop up.'

Again she disregarded that except for saying, 'Oddly enough Mount Serenity has taken on a personality for me. It's name is enough to calm one down, especially in the first days of getting the children into a schoolroom routine foreign to them. I find it very satisfying now, I don't know why I never took up teaching. Serenity's very shape, so perfectly symmetrical, has come to mean to me what Rangitoto Island used to mean, dead centre in the view from my window. When I'm bedevilled I run and look out of the window, and the sheer perfection of its cone and its cap of snow, with no rough rocks thrusting through like the other mountains, does something for me.'

'What kind of things bedevil you, Luenda?' he asked. 'You seem to have settled surprisingly well, but there

must be some things you miss horribly, especially after
working with a large staff of girls ... and men.' He put
his hand over hers as it lay on the table. Why she didn't
take hers away she didn't know.

When she didn't answer he said gently, 'Do you, after
all, miss Daryl?'

There was no hint of a too hasty denial, or of trying
to stop him probing. 'No, it was more than time that
was washed up. It was just a too comfortable rut we got
into. It's a mistake to drift like that, never to know the
real thing.'

His hand tightened. 'I think you were wise to
recognise that. One of my sisters was in the same box,
and Mother was married—she felt she might meet up
with it after she married this man, and make a mess of
things. But Rhonda recognised it herself in time and
had the courage to make the break, though if someone
hadn't had the grit to ask her if she knew where she was
heading, she'd have drifted on.'

Luenda looked up at him. 'And who did that? You?'
Her lips twitched. 'Because though I often admire your
straight speaking, you are inclined to be bossy, you
know. Oh, sure, you *are* the boss round here, but——'

He grinned. 'But sometimes I take too much upon
myself? I'm afraid I do. It becomes a habit. But it
wasn't me. At the time I was her kid brother. It was *her*
boss. He told her off, said she was aimless and for
goodness' sake to wake up!' The grin widened. 'Her
boss is now my brother-in-law.'

Luenda had to laugh. 'So it wasn't just a kindly
interest. But I like people who aren't afraid to act like
that.'

He changed the subject. 'Talking of Judy and her
riding lessons, you should speed up yours. I'd like you
really proficient before winter hardens the ground like
iron—makes a toss risky then. I'm taking over from
Wayne,' he added. 'He's going far too slowly. He's
enjoying them too—all that lifting of you down.'

A flake of anger appeared in her cheeks. 'I'm quite
capable of handling that myself, thanks. I took him to

task yesterday. I've met Wayne's kind before. He was just too affectionate at that lesson. I'm not, I repeat *not* encouraging him.'

Gwillym patted the hand under his. 'Calm down! I didn't accuse you of that, but I could tell, even at a distance, you were dealing with it. I saw you wag a forefinger at him after you pushed him away.'

'I'm glad you did, so leave it to me. There's no reason whatever for you to take over the lessons.'

'But there is . . . why should Wayne have all the fun?'

She snatched her hand from under his, stepped back and exclaimed, 'You hypocrite! I rather think I'll become very proficient speedily now . . . on my own! Let me tell you, big boss, I could just as easily smack your hand as his!' The brown eyes shot sparks at him.

He said, 'That's better. You've come alive. You've been too good to be true all these weeks—content with a round of domesticity, gardening, teaching. Wake up, Sleeping Beauty, there's more to life than that.'

He bent and kissed her, kissed her fiercely, lingeringly. Then he laughed and strode out as he heard Wilkie coming.

Luenda gathered up the twigs in the newspaper, and rushed headlong out of the back door to push them into the incinerator. Then she stood there, gazing across the fold of the green forested valley to where Mount Serenity rose from hundreds of acres of hill pasture. This morning even that failed to still within her this tide of awareness, this warm pulsing motion within her, in all her senses, body and spirit, a sweetness she'd not known before.

Gwillym wasted no time. That afternoon as soon as school was out he appeared, said, 'We'll have our three o'clock snack at two, Wilkie. I'm giving Luenda her lesson. Brent's got Wayne up with the others at Number One. They're repairing the sheep-pens.'

Wilkie looked surprised. 'That's a departure from custom, surely, you always start at Number Three Hut

way up, because the nearer the snowline the greater
priority.'

He was a little sharp with Wilkie for once. 'We can't
always work to a pattern. Number Three Hut means an
early start and an overnight stay. It suits me to have
them working on Number One for this half-day that's
free of other things. I'll make the tea,' he added, 'I see
the kettle's boiling. Kids, when we've had it I want you
to stack up the woodshed. Half the piles are
tumbledown. I want it done systematically, all the big
logs at the bottom, all the chips swept up and put in
cartons or the log-baskets. We'll be having more fires all
over the house this winter, with oil-fuel the price it is.
We've been asked to conserve it. When the pens are
finished at all the huts the men are going to get cracking
on the chain-saws. They'll tidy up all the trees they
felled last year, down by the fowlhouses.'

'Oh, beaut!' said Judith. 'Gwill, when they've done it,
can I have it fenced off? It used to be in the olden days
here, only the macrocarpas have bashed down the
netting. Then the fowls would lay their eggs in the nests.
We could let them out in the afternoons. They nearly
always lay before lunch. The runs are huge—or were.
It's an awful waste to find, like I did yesterday, nearly a
dozen eggs in the middle of a flax bush, all rotten. I put
them in a dish of water to test them and every one rose
and floated. Just because our wheat doesn't cost us
anything, it doesn't justify waste like that.'

His eyes softened as he looked at Judith. 'You're a
gem! You were made for a farmer's wife. You're right.
When we've got the time Steve and Dan are yours to
command. There can be a gate into the orchard for
them. They clean the ground under the trees of codlin
moth. You kids are sure acquisitions!' he grinned. 'The
stables are beginning to look like they were in Evan's
time, thanks to Di, and Davy's care of the dog motels is
something. Which brings me to something I've been
thinking of. You've proved you can work for sheer
enjoyment, now I'll put you on the payroll. I know your
sister gives you pocket-money, which you can't spend

here, but on your trips to Ludwigtown, you'll spend a lot all at once. What you earn here can pay for extras you crave for, for your hobbies, films and records and so on.'

Di's face wore a look of bliss. 'I want a new bridle for Lucky.' Davy, typically, said, 'It's going to take a long time to save for a trail-bike of my own, but I'll start right away.' They looked at Judith, the practical one, and she surprised them by saying, 'I want some new shoes—glam ones, not sensible ones, in case there's an evening party when we spend that week at the school.'

Gwillym said, 'Well, you'll be earning it, so you're entitled to spend it how you like ... within reason. Now, let's get cracking.'

As they walked to the paddock where the horse-jumps were, Luenda putting on her protective riding-helmet, she said, with a glance sideways, 'I hope Wayne wasn't aware of your reason for sending him off with the others. I hope you didn't make it obvious he was de-rated because of me. I'm quite capable of keeping him at a distance—of keeping anyone at a distance.'

He laughed. '*Are* you?' His glance was full of meaning and devilment.

She said quickly, 'You took me unawares. I watch for that sort of thing with Wayne and circumvent him with speed. He's so obvious. He's got far too much *amour*. He's effervescent and rather naïve with it, but I worked with such lashings of men, I never let it get out of hand.'

Gwillym disregarded that, saying, 'Wayne *was* well aware of my motives. He said, "You've got the dice loaded for you ... you're the boss. Not that I blame you, and I don't suppose she'll dare slap your face." And he rubbed his chin ruefully. I take it that was another time. Won't he keep his hands to himself?'

Luenda stopped in her walking, so that he stopped too, and swung round to face her. 'Look, Gwillym, I don't have to sneak on Wayne to you. I don't want him *or* you taking advantage of the riding lessons. It's simply stupid. All I aim to do is to catch up with Di's proficiency. I don't want her riding madly all over this

dangerous country with me trailing ineffectively behind.
I've conquered my worst fears. I was extremely nervous
at first, felt I'd far rather have gears and a driving-wheel
than be up that height, with a moving animal with a
mind of its own under me, but now I feel at one with
Dobby. She's not an exciting mount, but fine to go on
with. I want to concentrate, not be worried about
silly, amorous men. I need no help getting up or down.'

She expected him to look crushed, but he merely
grinned and said, 'Spoilsport! Looks as if I left my turn
a bit late.'

The brown eyes flashed. 'Gwillym Vaughan, you are
the most inconsistent man I've ever known! In
Auckland, before you had a chance to know me, you
warned me off. You wanted no feminine wiles up here.
You make me mad! Do you know what? It isn't always
the women who make the mischief, it's the stupid,
bumbling males! You can give me this one lesson so it
won't look as if we've quarrelled, then I'll just practise
in the paddock on my lone. I've got this far without
coming a cropper, so I'll be okay. Let me tell you
something . . . with you saying what you did to me in
Auckland the only man up here I'm really comfy with is
Claude. I just love him.'

He stared. 'Claude? Who—oh, how funny! You mean
old Dick Turpin. Wilkie told me you got on with him
like a house afire, but to call him Claude? I didn't think
anyone could get away with that. How come?'

'I just told him I thought he suited Claude for a
name.'

He burst out laughing. 'You'd make one of your
sudden remarks and get away with it! When your
thoughts sort of fizz to the top. Like my eyes being
green not brown, and saying, "Gwill, how on earth do
you shave that cleft in your chin?" Oh, Luenda, you *are*
a funny girl! You're so disarming. I picked you for
sophisticated, disturbing, ultra-feminine. It's disconcert-
ing. I have to keep changing my mind about you.'

She tried to hang on to the anger she'd felt a few
moments ago, but it was no good. 'Well, watch your

step just the same. I could be playing some deep deception of my own!'

Oh, what had possessed her to say that?

He took no notice, just pursued his own line of thought. 'I was so darned sure you'd cause havoc up here, like that other predatory female who nearly wrecked the boat up here—on another station—that it's a surprise to find you fitting in so well. Apart from Wayne, who, as you say, is much too amorous, you've been so natural, and you've twined Wilkie round your little finger and now old Dick's eating out of your hand. Claude indeed!'

'Well, I never see why anyone called Rhodes should automatically become Dusty Rhodes, or a girl whose surname is Turvey, like one I worked with once, always gets called Topsy,' said Luenda. 'Names are so important, so intimate. Now do let's get on with this lesson.'

Dobby came trotting up and nuzzled her shoulder. Luenda found she had more confidence today. Judith was going to graduate to another mount now. Perhaps *she* would soon. Gwillym was pleased.

After a while he opened a gate into a paddock where he had turned his own horse at lunch-time, and his Rollo came trotting up. 'You're doing well, Luenda. Good idea now to get used to another rider beside you, and practise wheeling round together.'

The wind blew back the short fair hair from her ears, whipped colour into the brown cheeks, and rippled the heavy cream silk shirt back against her. Something made her feel at one with her mount, with the whole terrain, the sound of the river purling over the mossy stones of the bed that was shallow here as it neared the lake. There were larks singing in the sky, though so high they were not visible, and sheep called from a hundred hills, all a blend of happiness. She even felt at one in the company of this man.

They crossed swords at times, which was to be expected, forced as they had been into unwilling partnership, a situation fraught with distrust and speculation, but when she could forget all that or disregard it as now, she found something kindred with him that she had never found with any other.

They rode up and down, wheeled, rode faster. It was exhilarating. Gwill said, 'Once more up to the far corner and back, then I think we could amble along the track—the lower one, towards Twin Hills. Just a mile or two.'

But as they neared the top fence it happened. All unseen by them, Samson, the big black rooster, had spotted, as he thought, Judith, his favourite, riding that horse he was so jealous of. He'd set off at a cracking pace along the fence-line at the side of them, his wings a little outspread to assist him, beak open in indignation. Luenda was nearest that fence.

Samson drew level, dived under the barbed wire and lifted his wings in a soaring motion that would have done credit to an eagle, uttering an eldritch shriek, and landed, claws scrabbling for a hold, on Dobby's fat rump.

She gave the most frightened whinny, tossed her head back, reared up and came down again with a thud, but at the same time managed to give a convulsive wriggle to dislodge this fearful demon that was clawing at her back. She also dislodged Luenda, who went flying over her head, across the fence, to land in the tussock at the other side.

Dobby's hoof lifted Samson clean back over the side fence. Gwillym was out of his saddle in a split second, under the fence and had reached Luenda, whose arms and legs were untangling themselves.

He expected her to be quite knocked out, thought the movement of her limbs quite automatic, but her startled face peered up at him as she flopped her arms back on each side of her. To his great relief she gasped, 'What was it? A hawk?'

He swore, and in the midst of the swearing she recognised Samson's name. She started to giggle weakly. He pulled himself together, said: 'Sorry for the language, I thought you'd be killed, Oh, Luenda, Luenda!'

To his own surprise he gathered her against him and pressed her head into his shoulder, patting her soothingly, murmuring words of comfort, all incoherent. He finished up, 'There, there! Don't tremble so.'

Her voice was indignant, she tried to sit up, 'Gwillym! I'm *not* trembling! I'm giggling.'

He peered into her face, 'So you are! Well, *I* don't feel like giggling. Worst of it is that if this had happened when Wayne was in charge, I'd have blistered him. As it is, I'll ring that damned bird's neck. He's a menace!'

Luenda sat up a bit more, still within the circle of his arms. 'You'll do nothing of the sort! It's just sheer affection on his part for Judith. But he must be shut in when we're riding. Mind you, he's probably had his lesson. I hope Dobby didn't hurt him. Oh, poor Dobby too. Look, she's taken off for the far gate.'

'Blast Dobby! It's not her I'm worried about. You *must* be hurt. But honestly, you're a natural. You gathered yourself into a sort of ball as you spun through the air and you missed everything, the wire, that ghastly *matagouri* bush, all thorns, and that rock. You landed clean in that tuft of tussock. But there must be skin off your back—turn over.'

'You don't need——' she began.

'Turn over.' She obeyed. Gwillym gently eased her shirt tail out and rolled it up to her neck. She winced as his cool fingers found a sore place on her left shoulder-blade, and a scratch nearby felt sticky and warm. But nothing deep. His hands went each side of her wasit, just above, where her ribcage was, exerted pressure.

'Tell me if you feel anything, but tell me quickly. If you've a cracked or broken rib, I don't want to push it in.' She arched her back a little, and his fingers probed further. She was glad he hadn't ordered her to turn over. She appreciated his delicacy of consideration in that.

His tone was relieved. 'I don't think you've done much harm, but you'll be mighty stiff tonight.'

'Possibly, but if I keep working this afternoon, it won't be too bad. Thanks, Gwillym.' She pulled her shirt down, stood up, with his help, and tucked it in, and suddenly gave way to real mirth.

He looked at her. 'I know what you're thinking: You're glad Wayne and the others aren't anywhere near. Goodness knows what they'd think if they saw this!'

'You got it in one, and explanations would sound so feeble.' She gave a gamin grin. 'I'm a great one for taking tumbles and coming to no harm. The kids would tell you that.'

He grinned back. 'Thanks—how reassuring! Next time I'll just shrug and walk away. But Luenda, one thing I must advise on.'

'Now, Gwillym,' she protested, 'that took me so by surprise I couldn't have acted on any advice. I don't suppose the book of rules for equestrians states what to do if a rooster suddenly lands on your horse's bottom!'

He said drily, 'My advice is that though coming from Auckland you probably didn't even own a singlet when you arrived, you buy yourself some in Ludwigtown for the coming winter. Even now, a bra and a silk shirt is ridiculous in this climate.'

Their shared laughter did them good.

The first weekend of the school holidays Gwillym and Wilkie, with the children, plus Brent and Josie and theirs, went to stay at Ludwigtown. The old goldmining settlement was crowded with tourists eager to revel in the lasting autumn sunshine, yet rejoicing in the sharp frosts of the mornings so there would be an early skiing and skating season.

Surprisingly Gwillym mentioned that he would stay on longer than the weekend, though Brent was taking just three days. Wilkie remarked on it with a wicked twinkle, which disturbed Gwillym not one bit, but Luenda pretended not to have heard. Wilkie looked smug at times, as if she was very satisfied that these two people she loved were finding kindred interests. They were, Luenda admitted to herself.

Here, in the little old cottage, Josie went out visiting at night, because she had a host of old school friends still living near. They encouraged her to do so because at Serenity, no wife would say, 'Well, this is my night off,' or take the car to a meeting or theatre. Josie knew the boys were all right with the others.

On Sunday, Gwillym said to Luenda, 'I'd like to go to the evening service. All the more so because the minister who's relieving here during the holidays used to be on Serenity. He was a cadet on the place when I was a youngster. He was by way of a hero to me—strong as an ox, a big fellow. I was playing up a bit—that resentment I told you about when Mum first remarried. Megan was making some headway with me, but boy, they were having a tough time. Bart Staines knocked some sense into me. Later he went into our theological college. I've only seen him once in the intervening years. Like to come with me, Luenda? Wilkie said she'd be fine here with the kids.'

Luenda found herself consenting. She had the odd feeling that the Gwillym she'd found so antagonising and disapproving in Auckland had disappeared and this was someone she was just getting to know.

It was going to be a cold night, already stars were pricking out and a crescent moon lit the sky to reveal the darker line of jagged peaks above the township huddled below in its dark pines. It was finger-tingling cold and even before darkness fell, their breath had been silver vapour on the air.

How different Gwillym looked tonight! He wore a grey suit, well cut, with a green shirt beneath it and a darker green tie, and he was shrugging himself into a gunmetal duffel coat. He looked at her. 'Luenda, you'd be far warmer in that scarlet coat with the hood with the white fur edging. It'll be really nippy coming home.'

She pulled a face. 'I feel rather like Santa Claus in it. Can't think why I ever bought it.'

'I like it. When you put it on for that walk up the hill I thought you looked like a Dickensian Christmas card.

You ought to wear it this winter when I've taught you to skate in Hazard Valley. By the time you come back to Serenity the ice should be hard enough up there and we'll start you on lessons. Before long you might be able to come to the rink over here.'

As she turned away to hook her coat down, her eyes gleamed with mischief. She'd do exactly what she'd planned when he first mentioned skating ... taking it for granted she'd be a duffer at that as well as at the riding. She'd let him put in an hour or so, she would feint a few stumbles, then suddenly she'd glide away from him and execute some of the figures that had gained her those cups. She'd sworn the children to secrecy. They thought it would be a great lark.

It *was* cold. Their footsteps rang on the hard ground where pinpoints of frost already gleamed. The path led up under the branches of giant trees planted by pioneers in the long ago, to break the pitiless force of the winds that howled up the gorges.

Gwillym said, looking down suddenly, 'Luenda, how daft! You haven't got gloves on. It's freezing, girl. I know you wouldn't wear them in Auckland, but I saw Wilkie give you a pair to bring over here.'

She said simply, 'They're purple, they'd clash with scarlet.'

He laughed indulgently. 'Women! As if it mattered against elements like this.'

She shrugged. 'I've a pocket this side. That hand's warm.'

Gwillym reached out, took the cold hand that hung between them, and thrust it, still inside his, into the huge pocket of his duffel.

'That's better,' she said, and was annoyed to hear a tremble in her voice. She hoped he wouldn't read into it that quick, betraying physical response she felt. She'd never before been so vitally aware of a man. Pleasurably thrilled sometimes, yes, at the odd goodnight kiss, but never had she known this demanding blood-leaping urgency for more and closer contact. What *was* she thinking? How could she, when she knew that any advances this man made to her were only the product of expediency, all with the dollar sign on them? How that hateful phrase kept cropping up in her mind, to jeer at her for these tender feelings she could not control. Well, he'd see. Just as it was going to be fun to score over him in the matter of skating, so it would satisfy something within her, something that hurt, when, for the sake of the possible inheritance of half the estate, he sought her in marriage. What a shock he'd get when she turned him down! Just as well Fenella had warned her. Poor Fenella!

The little stone church, like the cottage, was whitewashed, with blue sills and frames. Its bell was tolling out with silver deeps in the clear snell air. The rime was even glinting on the pine-needles. They went in. The church was almost full.

As they sat down, the same calmness Luenda knew when she gazed on Mount Serenity fell upon her, engulfing and stifling all these unworthy thoughts. She looked up at the brass tablet above them. It said:

> 'In loving memory of Myfanwy and Evan Richards
>   lake-dwelling pioneers
>   of Mount Serenity
> who through many vicissitudes, natural
> disasters and great happiness laid
> the foundations of prosperity here
>   for generations to come.'

Luenda looked down quickly, to hide the tears that rushed to her eyes. She was aware Gwillym had followed her look upwards. His hand touched hers in her lap, fleetingly. 'Gets you, doesn't it?'

She nodded, whispering back, 'Gives you a great sense of continuity. In town churches the past is peopled with so many folk, and they move about so, they get lost sight of.'

'I always sit here if I can. Ah, here's Bart.' The vestry door had opened and the session clerk ushered in the Reverend Bartholomew Staines in his black Geneva gown, white linen bands lying on the black stock under his chin.

There was magic in the service from beginning to end. For the first time since her mother had died, Luenda felt a sense of security. Bart spoke of the stillness in the heart of the storm, of the soul stayed upon God. She had a flash of inspiration. . . . He ought to finish up with Rupert Brooke's poem. It seemed inevitable. It was.

'. . . Safe shall be my going,
    Secretly armed against all death's endeavour;
Safe through all safety's lost; safe where men fall;
    And if these poor limbs die, safest of all.'

It was good to witness the meeting between Bart and Gwillym. Men had a way of meeting after a long time of not seeing each other, something that put time and distance at nothing. Bart said, 'I was going to ring the Station tomorrow to see if we could come across during the week. How splendid to have you actually this side of the lake. We're here for a whole fortnight, occupying the manse. Can you come in for supper, man?' His eye flicked to Luenda at Gwillym's elbow. 'And . . .?'

Gwillym brought her forward. 'This is my partner, Luenda Morgan.'

Her hand was engulfed in Bart's huge paw, and he said, 'We'll be delighted if you'll come too.'

She said quickly, 'I could just go on home—we're at the cottage. You'll have so much to talk about.'

The Reverend Bartholomew shook his head. 'I meant that word, delighted. For a moment, seeing you together, I hoped your name might be Vaughan, but we'll be glad to have Gwill's partner. Sounds a new development for Serenity. Stand in the porch till I see the rest of the congregation, it's too cold outside. My wife's not out yet. Ah, here she is—Janet, Gwill and his partner, one Luenda Morgan.'

Seemingly Gwill had met Janet that one time, shortly after they were married. Since then, they'd lived in northern manses. Presently they walked a block to the manse, set in huge grounds at the far end of Church Lane. Beyond it, against the dark hills, glimmered the white of tall tombstones. Bart waved a hand. 'Fascinates me—always did. I know half the histories, and I wish I knew the other half. Many of them were unknown, miners from the Californian gold-rush, others from Bendigo in Australia, some from the ends of the earth. It's doubtful if all of them are buried under their own names. Their relatives might never have known where they ended up. And now Ludwigtown is such a settled community, largely fifth generation farmers.'

Gwill had a strange note in his voice. 'But sometimes fresh blood comes in, and is good for all of us.'

Bart said quickly, 'That's so, Gwill. It got into your blood from the start, didn't it? As if you'd been born and bred to it. Mount Serenity was your place, and of course Evan and Megan recognised that.'

Gwill said, 'That wasn't all I meant, but it's true. Luenda and the youngsters have somehow made Serenity come alive again. We were getting very stodgy.'

Janet Staines' voice squeaked with surprised. 'Luenda . . . I mean Mrs Morgan . . . you don't look old enough to have youngsters!'

Gwillyms voice was full of laughter. 'Appearances are deceptive. Janet, Di and Judy are twelve, Davy ten.'

'I don't believe it,' Janet protested.

He relented then. 'You don't have to strain your credulity that far—they're her sisters and brother. Well, halfs . . . like me, her mother married again. She's their guardian.'

Janet fetched him a crack with her hymn-book. 'Today's been full of surprises. I recognised you at once, in spite of having met you only once, so long ago, and I made up my mind in church that you'd renounced bachelorhood at last.'

'Here, what's this at last business? I'm only thirty-two!'

'Well, you oughtn't to be,' said Janet crossly. 'I mean, you oughtn't to be still a bachelor, and raising my romantic hopes.'

Luenda decided to pay Gwillym out. 'Instead of which,' she chuckled, 'with Gwill and myself it wasn't a case of love at first sight, but instant loathing.'

'Whatever can you mean? What did you do? Run into his car or something?'

Gwill said, 'Impossible. I don't have a car—no roads. Only tracks for Land Rovers and tractors.'

Luenda said, 'It was much worse than that. I was a disaster—I was foisted on to him as a sort of partner, by Mrs Richards. She was repaying what she thought was a debt to my grandfather. She had no thought, apparently, of the bombshell effect I was to have on the peaceful existence of Mount Serenity . . . bringing three city children and a dog down here. But it's only for a year, then we'll leave him in peace once more. Just a ripple on the surface of the lake, then gone for ever.'

Gwillym's voice was deliberate. 'Ripples widen till they reach the edge. And a year of ripples could affect the lake-shore.'

Nobody said anything. Then Bart said, 'Ah, here we are, it's a long dark drive. I ought to have brought a torch.'

Gwillym's hand found Luenda's elbow. 'Green-eyed people see farther than others in the dark,' he said softly.

Janet's mother had been baby-sitting for their children, and had a roaring fire of blue-gum logs and pine-cones on, and there was laughter and warmth and sheer affection in the atmosphere as Gwill and Bart began to recall old times. Luenda had a feeling of unreality. She felt a different girl from the one who had entered the church.

It was as if in entering she had slipped from her former existence into a new life, a complete acceptance of the change in her circumstances. As she realised it, she felt suddenly afraid. Was she wise in letting the distrust she'd known of Gwillym Vaughan and his motives slip away from her? Wasn't it a safeguard? But how impossible to equate Gwill's attitude tonight with a man who'd plot coldbloodedly to gain complete ownership of a property. A man who would break another girl's heart to do that!

Two hours later they were walking home through that silver radiance of starlight, moonlight and frost-sparkle, a dangerous alchemy. Her hand was warm inside his pocket again, his hand engulfing hers.

They passed a street corner. Gwillym said, 'That's where the skating rink is. We'll come over when they hold the championships. They're worth coming for. You might be able to enter in for one of the novice competitions by then.'

That did it. She said swiftly, 'Gwillym, do you ever find that going to church resolves things for you? A certain way of behaviour, say?'

His hand tightened on hers. 'Why, Luenda, isn't that what it's supposed to do? People find themselves forgiving slights, or deep hurts, or quarrels. Also they sometimes find their problems are resolved *for* them. Something bugging you?'

'It was, but not now. You won't like me for this, but I can't help that. I've got to tell you. It's so petty now, I can't think why I ever let it matter.'

'Tell me. Whatever it is, it needn't matter. *I'm* rather ashamed now of the way I reacted in Auckland. I judged you on the strength of your appearance done up to the nines and in a dress too low. And you'd taken on as a substitute, because your boss was under strain. I shan't go up in righteous indignation, whatever you've done.'

He pulled her to a stop, stepped with her under a great spreading macrocarpa, thick with shelter. He brought her round to face him, holding her by the elbows. Through a broken branch, a gleam of the moonlight fell on her serious face, framed by the red hood with the white fur.

'Right?'

Luenda said slowly, 'When I went into church I thinking of doing such a petty thing, in which I was going to score off you. I felt very much the city greenhorn when we came here . . . couldn't ride, didn't know the difference between wethers and rams, and even the children knew that ... I thought you had to have a rooster before hens would lay eggs ... I've given you a lot of laughs. So when you assumed you'd have to teach me to skate, I was as mad as a meat-axe. I decided not tell you I was almost a champion ice-skater. I was going to let you teach me, simulating nervousness and spills, then all of a sudden I was going to glide away from you, doing all sorts of intricate figures ... flying camels, an effortless axle, a flip and a half, a sit-spin ... and you were going to be really crestfallen. It was *rotten* of me. I've—I've even got cups for skating!'

For a moment she felt the vials of his wrath were about to fall upon her. His grip tightened till it hurt, then he burst out laughing. 'And serve me damned well right too! Oh, Luenda, Luenda, you're so funny ... you've got all the spirit in the world to get flaming mad and think up something like that ... poetic justice really, but you've got too much integrity to carry it out. You funny, *dear* thing!'

He pulled her close, bent his head, brought his mouth down upon hers, seeking, demanding, and getting response. She was so thankful he wasn't furious, she clung gratefully. Suddenly she felt she was overdoing the response. She tried to draw back.

He said indignantly, 'What are you trying to do now? Look, we've had very few moments without misunderstanding till now, or few even alone. Don't you think this is nice?'

In spite of herself she chuckled. 'Well, yes. I mean perhaps.'

'There's no perhaps about it. It *is* nice.'

She said, 'I—I—but I think we were getting just a bit carried away by suddenly declaring a truce. Gwillym, let me breathe, I want to talk.' She moved her lips away again.

'I can't think why. This is much more enjoyable than talking.' His tone was audacious. 'Well, you *can* talk for a little while. After all, I can enjoy kissing you here ... and here ... and here.' He laughed. 'And now you've forgotten what you wanted to say. So what's the good of letting your lips go?'

She sighed, said severely, 'No wonder I've forgotten! No, Gwill, let me go on talking.'

'Okay, and while you're talking I'll just undo that great thick jacket. Don't misunderstand or I'll beat you. I can't get anywhere near you with that on. It's like trying to kiss a grizzly bear, fur and all!'

Luenda was conscious of that feeling of one's bones turning to water, which till now she'd thought a ridiculous phrase whenever she had read it. She ought to resist that feeling; how could she be sure of this man? But . . . but it *was* nice.

He slipped his hands around her waist under the coat and linked them behind her, so she was held in embrace, but not too tightly.

'All right, you funny little thing, what did you want to say?'

She stumbled a bit. 'I know what I mean, but I'm not sure if the words will come out right, Gwill.'

His voice was actually tender, but amused. 'No, because I've rather taken your breath away, after our former hostility.'

He meant it literally. She took it in an abstract way. 'I'll say! It's too big a change to take in all at once. I— You're going too fast, Gwillym. I think the romantic atmosphere tonight got you. Such a happy couple, the Staines,' she tried to change the subject. 'So keen on linking you up with someone. You could feel so different tomorrow in the cold light of day. Besides, it's all been too much—such a prickly situation, positively bristling with difficulties. I mean, being pitchforked together on the estate at the whim of a woman who liked us both and felt she could play God. So we had this terrible antagonism. Now suddenly there's this . . . this . . .'

He supplied the word. 'This closeness?'

'Yes, that'll do. Although it's not quite right . . . this *seeming* closeness. But I think for your own sake I've got to head you off. I've got the responsibility of three

children, and . . . and there were things in my immediate
past that disturbed me so much emotionally. That final
reckoning from Megan hangs over our heads too.
Perhaps it doesn't worry you as much as it worries me.'

'That needn't worry you,' said Gwillym.

'Oh, that's absurd! To have that hanging over me for
twelve months is ghastly,' she protested. 'Oh, all right,
only ten months now. But life at Serenity is giving me a
breathing-space I needed badly. I haven't half the
problems I'd have had in Auckland.'

'You mean that these days a city that size isn't the
easiest in which to manage teenagers?'

She hesitated, 'Well, that's some of it, I suppose.' She
couldn't tell him that the greatest problem of all would
be managing financially. That dollar sign again!

Gwillym drew her close again, comfortingly, without
passion. 'And it helps, having Wilkie and myself in the
same house?'

'I expect that's it. Mount Serenity Station is a haven
to me just now. But I mustn't allow myself to be too
much influenced by——'

He laughed. 'By moments like these?'

Luenda looked up at him and in the faint light he saw
her lips tremble. 'Please, Gwillym?'

He slackened his hold, but not entirely. She saw the
corners of his mouth quirk up and momentarily a
positive wave of love swept over her. It left her weak.
He said gently, 'I did get carried away. I'll back off a bit
if you like. I don't usually rush my fences, only I was
so . . .' He changed his mind. 'I won't finish that. It
would carry me right to the other side of the fence, and
I don't think you're ready to take it. But I'm not
backing off *too* far. Let's just stand here for a moment,
like this.' He put his cheek against hers. It was faintly
rough, comfortingly masculine.

In a gesture of thanks Luenda put her hand to his
other cheek. She knew she would always remember this.
There was such security in his warmth, in his hard
strength. Why, oh, why couldn't the circumstances of
their meeting have been ordinary? It could have

happened that instead of the clashes, the distrust, the
money motives that being forced together in an
unwelcome partnership had entailed, it could have been
that if Megan Richards had come back from Los
Angeles instead of dying over there, she might have
wanted Luenda to go down to Serenity for a holiday. It
would have been simple, uncomplicated. The magic of
what might have been swept over her.

Presently Gwillym said in a very ordinary tone, 'Now
we finish our walk home. Button up your coat and put
your hand in my pocket.'

The house was all in darkness—tactful of Mirabel.
They went through the little front door, and paused. He
said, 'Thank you for telling me what you'd planned to
do about the skating. Brave of you.' She stood
irresolute, not knowing on what note to end this strange
evening.

Gwillym resolved it for her. 'You can see your way to
your room by the landing light, can't you?' He bent his
head, brushed her lips lightly with his, pinched her chin
and said, 'Sleep now, and sweet dreams, Luenda. We've
got time ahead of us, remember that.'

She didn't lie awake. No analysing tonight. Some
hours were too happy for that. And who knew what the
future might yet hold?

CHAPTER SEVEN

THURSDAY Gwillym went back across the lake. They all trooped down to see him off. He was loaded up with the results of their shopping plus, as he said, a half-ton of library books and newly-bought books, and freshly-made cakes that Wilkie had whipped up the night before. Gwillym had protested, 'The deep-freeze is full of stuff you and Luenda baked earlier.'

'Well, this is in case Dick's forgotten to take some out to thaw like I told him. This is just to stay your stomachs till the other's thawed.'

He chuckled, 'Oh Wilkie, there's enough here to feed one of the old-time shearing gangs! You were supposed to be having a complete break.'

'I am having it. A smaller house, and a girl like Luenda to keep me company. Just imagine, I might have got one like Fenella.'

Fenella! Since that first night when Wayne had brought Fenella's letter she'd never been mentioned. Though of course she hadn't lived at Serenity, but at Twin Hills.

So it was true what that girl had said, forlornly, that Wilkie detested her. Some clash of personalities, Luenda supposed, though Mirabel was normally the most understanding and tolerant person Luenda had known. Wilkie said to Luenda, 'Fenella was a disaster wished on to Marie Campion as a governess by the Labour Office. A girl devoted to the three M's . . . Men, Money, Marriage.'

Luenda stared. It was the first catty remark she'd ever heard from the housekeeper. As Gwill had once said, she'd find an excuse for the very devil himself. Mirabel caught her look and burst out laughing. 'I've shocked Luenda! Dear girl, while I usually fly to the defence of my own sex, there has to be an exception.

124

Fenella was the most predatory female I'd ever met and she put my back up and my claws out. But praise be, she's safely back in Australia and not likely to be back. At least not on our side of the lake!'

Luenda couldn't resist a quick look at Gwillym's face, but as usual, that dark countenance gave nothing away. Not that she thought it forbidding now. It could be whimsical and tender ... the memory of the way he had kissed her visited her with sweet recall ... at that moment he looked up from slapping masking tape on one of the cartons and caught her eye. He smiled at her instantly. In that moment she felt they shared a world of two and it seemed as if her heart did a double somersault. She looked away quickly, not wanting even Wilkie to see that exchange of looks.

She caught with a desperate hope at Wilkie's words about Fenella. *Had* she been like that? Had Gwillym too been glad when the Tasman Sea lay between them? Yet she had seemed so sincere, so desolated. Luenda shut her mind to the picture of a forlorn Fenella. They all went down in the local taxi with the stuff, a taxi of the station wagon type that they used a lot in this area for loading launches.

The usual things were said in the last few minutes. Gwillym said, 'Well, make the most of your time, all of you. There won't be another break for a while, only don't let this gay metropolis unsettle you for the solitary life on Serenity.'

The girls giggled madly at this mild humour. 'Twenty shops,' they said. 'We counted them! Don't worry, Gwill darling, wild horses wouldn't get us away from Serenity. You're stuck with us, did you know?'

He pulled a face. 'I was frightened of this. Well, I'll stop crossing the days off my calendar now till your departure.'

Wilkie said with satisfaction, 'Megan knew what she was about when she brought this family to Moana-Kotare.'

Luenda groaned. 'Those twins have never heard that silence is golden! They embarrass me a dozen times a day. Anybody would think there's no other existence but at Serenity.' She had to say it. She couldn't have Wilkie or anybody else thinking they were digging in. The future was too uncertain, dependent upon the whim of a benefactress who could have had some eccentric notion to perpetrate.

The children and Wilkie had turned away to watch a hovercraft coming towards the jetty. Gwillym looked up, said in a low voice, '*Is* there any other existence, Luenda?'

The colour rose in her cheeks. 'A good many people must think so, Gwill. Millions, in fact.'

'I meant for us. For you, Luenda?'

She looked down, said rather shakily, 'I think the only answer to that—at present—is no comment.'

'At present?' She could sense the smile in his voice. 'That's better than a quick denial, anyway. I hope you mean what I think you mean.'

She had to say something, so she said hurriedly, 'I mean we haven't experienced the winter yet.'

The laugh in his voice was more pronounced now. 'Oh, you were thinking of the weather?'

'Yes, of course.'

'Then the forecast's good, girl, it was a stormy out-look to start with, but it's set fair now. Remember that.'

Luenda didn't reply. He sensed the excited talk about the hovercraft was dying down and added in a very low voice, 'I said if you wanted to make the most of it over here, to give me a ring not to come if you wanted to stay the second week, but . . . would it be selfish of me to say I hope you won't?'

She forgot she'd told him to rein in and heard herself say, 'It's a nice thing to say, Gwill. Makes me feel less of an interloper.'

Nothing more could be said then. She was astounded at how bereft she felt as the wake of the launch dwindled into nothingness across the sheen of the blue-green waters. Three whole days before he came back for them.

It was strange to be able to collect mail every day from their private bag at the Post Office, and the children spent hours in the evenings answering letters from their friends in Auckland. Luenda was thankful the letters didn't trigger off any homesickness for life as it used to be. It was obvious the children had written in glowing terms of life as lived on the Serenity run. In fact they'd probably been insufferable as they described the sheer adventure of living beyond the reach of roads.

Wilkie had just put a letter aside from her daughter till she read her other mail. 'I've always saved the icing on the cake till last. Jenny writes so vividly of Queensland it's nearly as good as a visit.'

Luenda knew Jenny lived in Australia, that her husband was with a scenic airline, but she detected a note almost of nostalgia in Mirabel's voice. Perhaps it just meant she longed to visit Jenny. She said, 'I take it Jenny's husband is a New Zealander?'

Mirabel looked surprised. 'Did I never say? No, he's an Australian.' Luenda had time only to blink in surprise when Mirabel added, 'From my very own state too, Queensland.' Then she asked, 'What are you boggling for, Luenda?'

Luenda said, dazed, 'I took you for a born-and-bred Kiwi.'

Mirabel burst out laughing. 'I mean to say, why all the surprise? I lost my accent because I was only twelve when Dad came back to New Zealand to live. He was born here. I thought the end of the world had come. I missed the heat and the warm seas, our incomparable beaches. I reckon I was homesick for Australia for eight years. Till I married Jock at twenty.'

Her voice softened as it always did when she mentioned Jock, Jock the love of her life who had been dead for more than fifteen years. They talked on. Mirabel was charmed to know that Luenda's stepfather had taken them all to Surfers' Paradise for a holiday some years ago. Then Wilkie said, 'Well, I'd better read her letter now.' She didn't scan more than a few lines before she flung it down and said in tones as excited as if she'd been as young as the twins, 'Oh, how wonderful! You'll never guess. . . Greg, Jenny's husband, has got a job with a firm in Queenstown here, scenic flying. They'll be here in two months' time!' She read on, then looked even more excited if that were possible, 'Oh, and they're going to have a baby. They thought it wasn't possible for her to have one . . . but she is. I thought I wouldn't be a grandmother till Marian got married. Oh, how glad I am for them! Luenda, just imagine, they'll be just half an hour's drive from Ludwigtown. Oh, Greg came here for an interview but didn't dare ring in case it raised hopes that might be dashed. Listen to this: "Mum, you said Megan had left you the cottage. Any chance of us having it for a few weeks, possibly less, while we house-hunt in Queenstown? Of course if you hear of any suitable house for sale in Queenstown itself, I'd fly over like a shot. Don't let anything likely to charm us, pass by. And Mum, won't it be marvellous when at last you retire, to have you half an hour's drive from your grandson or granddaughter?

"You'd better book me in at the Queenstown maternity hospital pronto. For December 14th, probably. Isn't that clever of us? I'll have my baby home for Christmas. Any chance of you retiring by then? Haven't you worked long enough? Give Gwill a prod in the right direction—it's time he brought a bride to Serenity. Tell him I said so. He'd have been married long since had he not been looked after far too well by you and Megan. Try neglecting him." '

Wilkie chuckled. 'That girl! Men don't marry for housekeepers. Sometimes they marry for money, I suppose, or where money is, but even if the way to a man's heart is through his stomach, I don't really think they marry for that.'

A chill finger touched Luenda's heart, stilling the joy she had known on Sunday night, and in those precious moments before the boat left. *They don't marry for housekeepers . . . but sometimes they marry for money.* For money *or land*.

She received quite an astonishing amount by cheque

from the solicitor and spent some joyously, loving being able to shop for the girls and Davy in the matter of thicker winter clothing, and not having to count every penny. For herself too.

On the day of return she was wearing one new outfit as they piled out of the taxi at the jetty. Gwillym had beaten them to it by a few seconds. It was an emerald green trouser suit in herringbone tweed, with a scarlet polo-necked sweater under it, something that lit up the brown eyes and the coral of her cheeks, and in deference to the cold wind blowing across the vivid lake from the snowy heights above it, a white woollen head-square was tied over her head. She fancied a light of appreciation leapt into Gwill's eyes as he took a bound on to the wharf. Three figures came up from the cabin, each with a weekend bag—Stephen, Dan, Wayne.

Wayne was grinning, 'The boss is so pleased to have you back he's giving us a few days off in Dunedin. We're flying down. Reckons that seeing it's school holidays he can get you four yarding and drafting. Wish you joy of it. I don't remember this ever happening before. Reckon he wants you to himself, Luenda, cunning hound! Save some of your favours till I return!'

Gwillym buffeted Wayne on the shoulder in answering vein, but Luenda had an idea he didn't much like it. The three went off, eager to be on their way. 'How are they getting to Frankton airport?' asked Luenda. 'They should have grabbed that taxi.'

'Oh, Wayne has a friend who's going to run them over in his car.'

They stowed their stuff and headed out across the lake, with Mount Serenity centring their passage like a lodestar. Luenda was amazed at the exhilaration that possessed her. She came to stand beside Gwillym at the wheel. 'Does Claude ever take a few days off?' she asked.

'Not apart from his annual holiday, which he takes when it suits him and always goes to his sister at Picton. He sometimes comes with us if we come for just the day. He never stays. He's a secretive old bounder, you know. But he must have friends in Arrowtown, because he always gets a taxi and goes off there. Never says a word about it.'

'Well, it's an interesting spot, full of gold-mining history, and he worked there a year or two as a young man,' said Luenda.

Gwill looked at her in astonishment. 'Did he? Did he tell you himself or did you discover it?'

'He told me.'

'Well, I'm blest! Compared with Old Dick, I've always thought a clam would be a positive babbler. He's been here upwards of forty years and I don't reckon anyone on the station knew that. Dad—my stepfather—was manager here for ages and he never said. But you've been here less than two months and know all about him.'

'Not all. And I never asked any questions. He just volunteered it.'

'When, for goodness sake—when?'

'Mostly just after school. He sometimes comes over then. You know how the kids dash out helter-skelter? I stay in for a bit tidying up and setting lessons for next day, doing the blackboard stuff and so on, and Claude often drops in then. He's interested in the lessons, you know, especially the English ones. Not the grammar but the literature.'

'I knew he's a great reader,' said Gwillym, 'he always calls at the library here when he comes, but this is news to me.'

'Wilkie knows, but she never interrupts. She said if she came in, he'd not say a word.'

His hand left the wheel, touched hers briefly. 'You needn't be on the defensive, Luenda. I'm tickled pink. He gets on my conscience a bit. I often used to ask him over when the chaps were coming across for cards, but he'd never come. Not even when we've had much older fellows working here and living in the same house with him. He doesn't bother much with TV even. We put that one in the living-room for the lads, and got Dick a portable for himself, so he could pick his own programmes, but he's not an addict—prefers reading, and likes his radio programmes, the ones he's listened to for an age.'

He laughed. 'This explains the message he gave me for you. I had a hard job concealing my surprise when he said to me this morning, "Ask Luenda to come to see me after dinner tonight. She did an errand for me while she was away." '

He looked questioningly at her, and a little smile touched her lips. 'Yes, I did. I've to report—and Gwill, I hope it won't set you back, but it's—well, rather private to Claude. I'd like to tell you, but——'

'I won't get huffy. We all have our little secrets, and do you know what? I like a woman who can keep her counsel, especially about other people's business. By the way, Luenda, I saw you pay the taxi—there's no need for that. I should have told you. We use him a lot, dashing over to Queenstown or Arrowtown, and have an account with him. The estate pays it, all part of the service, even the lads can if they need it. Compensates for being so isolated if they aren't dependent upon infrequent buses on their days off. I'll reimburse you.'

She said instantly: 'No, thanks. I like to be a little independent. I did know it could be charged because Mirabel said, but I find I'm taking such a generous allowance from the station, and it's heavenly, after having to be so cheeseparing for so long, to be able to afford to do so.'

She'd said it without thinking. Gwillym swung round from the wheel, said, 'Cheeseparing? Weren't you left well off? I mean, that house in one of Auckland's best bays, two cars sold, a boat, and everything in the house was so choice—not opulent, but quite frankly, nothing hinted of having to scratch and scrape.'

Luenda didn't feel upset at having given herself away. This new Gwillym would understand. He no longer resented her. She said in a low voice, 'Gwill, I'll tell you later. The children could come rushing over.'

He accepted that. The children got excited as they neared. He chuckled, 'I was afraid that being over at the little old burg might have unsettled them, but I needn't have worried. Luenda, you were fortunate in this . . . you could have had a helluva time if the kids had hated it here.'

She nodded. 'I know. That I dreaded and needn't have. But at first it was the one compensation.'

'Compensation for what?'

Her voice was reluctant. 'I keep on saying things without thinking. But it doesn't seem to matter now, I don't think you'll feel I'm trying to reproach you. You see, our finances had had a severe reverse. It was terribly traumatic coming to live where we were not wanted, when I was pre-judged as being on the make. Megan Richards didn't know from me, but you thought I'd made the most of my opportunities with her.'

His voice held real regret. 'I know. That must have been a worse hell—to feel unwanted.'

She said quickly, 'Gwill, don't feel bad about it. I know what it looked like. I couldn't bear you to feel like that.'

His mouth relaxed. 'Generous of you. I appreciate that. To hark back to that Sunday night . . . do you remember still that phrase in Bart's prayer we both liked? "Forgive what was said amiss," and I have a lot to ask you to forgive me for. Then he said, "Confirm what was said aright." I've a lot to confirm, only you want me to take it slowly. But do remember I'm not a patient man.'

They put about and glided up to the scarlet jetty, their bow breaking up the early winter reflections in the stillness of the water. Everything had been double, splotches of scarlet and russet and gold from the last of the autumn trees, two jetties, all the small boats floating double, the bright red roof of the woolshed . . . all made a picture to be etched upon the heart for ever. Had there ever been a lovelier place to return to?

Luenda lifted her face towards her mountain in a moment of deep thankfulness, not for just a roof over their heads, but for the promise that a brighter future was to be theirs. Misunderstandings were dissolving like the mountain mists that clung lovingly round Mount

Serenity in these early mornings till, as now, the sun dispersed them.

Gwill gave a shout of laughter. 'Can you beat that? There's Dick down at the jetty to meet us! Wonders'll never cease. I don't know what's come over this place.'

Behind him Wilkie said, 'Don't you know, Gwill?'

He glanced quickly at Luenda and the children, who were all at the rail now, and said softly, 'I *do* know, Wilkie.'

Her beautiful blue eyes sparkled. 'Then get a move on, lad. I never thought you'd be a laggard!'

He looked indignant. 'I'm not. I'm raring to go, but Luenda told me to slow the pace. What do you take me for? Well, come on, Dick's only just holding Griff in. He'll leap on the boat soon, and probably miss and take a ducking. Hey, Davy, watch it, or you'll be the one to get wet, and the water's icy!'

Dick actually came up to the house with them and had a cup of tea. Then he said with a grin, 'The boys'd like to have been here to show Judith something now it's finished, so I'm to do the honours. Come on!'

They all trooped after him, though Gwillym, of course, had already seen it. They went through the big iron gate out of the garden, and under large gums and macrocarpas, where they saw signs of great clearance. Here Dick stopped and clapped his hands over Judy's eyes, walked her on, then, when they'd turned a bend in the track, took his hands away.

She stopped stock-still, then to everyone's surprise, instead of rushing forward to the new hen-houses, turned and flung herself at Claude Turpin, arms going up round his neck, and gave him a whopping kiss. Claude bore it with surprising equanimity, laughing.

The men had made a wonderful job of it. They'd covered the old boards with rough-barked, half-split timber, so it looked like a palisade in the Canadian backwoods, put new iron on the roofs, made doors that shut instead of sagging, installed new nestboxes that could open from the outside with no disturbance to any laying hen, and the runs were perfect because they'd built them round a couple of smaller trees, so the fowls still had plenty of shade and room for perching for the hot days of the Central Otago summer. The drinking troughs could be filled from the outside and there was a small new building away from the others. 'My idea and my workmanship,' said Claude proudly, 'that's for broody hens and chicks. Smaller-mesh wire, and it's in three stages. They'll be really safe from predators there.

'And the boss got his wish for access to the orchards for them. That gate leads in. And Wilkie, we patched up the orchard fence so they can't get into your flower garden or your herb garden. And they've still got over half an acre to roam in.'

Over the door of the main fowl-house Stephen had painted a great sign, with fluffy yellow chicks on it, that read 'Judy's Hen Ranch'. Judith went inside the runs, and sure enough, every single fowl squatted down to be stroked.

Luenda and Gwillym brought up the rear as they marched back to the house. He looked at Luenda. 'Another invisible bond woven,' he said.

She had a query in her eyes.

He gestured towards Judith. 'Something more to bind you to this station. I expect you dreaded the upheaval for them, in case they hated it, the isolation, the tearing apart of their normal existence. But I honestly think it would be as nothing to how they'd feel now if you took them away from here.'

Luenda bit her lip. 'I know.'

Gwill frowned. 'What's that look for? You don't want to go back to city life, do you?'

She said slowly, 'Gwillym, it's not a clear-cut issue. I don't know what Megan had in mind for me . . . finally. At present I'm only a sort of partner in the estate. It's just for a year, a trial year. There are things I dread about that final revelation.'

He shrugged. 'I don't. Whichever way the cookie crumbles, it'll suit me. So I don't dread anything.'

A little angered, she said, 'Of course you don't. Half the estate was left you by Megan, so there's no problem. I have this odd feeling that Megan had something up her sleeve none of us may suspect.'

His fingers gripped her arm just below the elbow. 'Luenda, I'm sorry it was this way. It's something I can't do a thing about—yet. To relieve your mind, I mean. At least, though, I knew Megan well, and I'm sure anything she had in mind will be best for both—for all of us.'

Luenda felt all her old doubts surge back. Why, she didn't know. She found it so hard to believe it was all coming right. Was she being a fool to let all caution go? Was this man merely disarming her? Had he a pretty shrewd idea of what had been in Megan's mind? Was he taking full advantage of whatever it was? Was he just pretending he didn't know? It could be that Megan had talked it over with Gillian, and Gillian might have told Gwillym.

Mentally she made a wild clutch at her former doubts and mistrust. What had come over her that she had reversed them so quickly? Fenella had been pretty sure half the estate was to come to Luenda, and only Gwillym could have told her that. She mustn't succumb to his charm, his kindredness, his thoughtfulness, even his remorse at having resented her so at first.

But the suspicions were hard to maintain in the face of the sheer pleasure of their homecoming. The tranquil old house folded its peace about Luenda . . . she felt she had always known those worn treads on the stairs where the carpet sank into the hollows made by generations of feet, the little window on the landing that framed Mount Serenity, the funny old range that purred such a welcome with its steaming iron kettle and its soup-pot bubbling away. Gwillym must have thawed out from the deep-freeze some of Wilkie's mutton-broth.

The cats looked as if they hadn't stirred from the old rag rug since they went away. Goldie was still eternally washing her immaculate coat . . . Gwill had once said he couldn't imagine how she could work up enough spit for this perpetual motion! And John Halifax, Gentleman, usually called Hallie for short, looked more

Victorian than ever in his black and white coat, with the markings round his mouth that looked exactly like a waxed moustache.

Time stood still here. It was not only the charm of a dark-browed, lilting-voiced Welshman that disarmed you, it was the tempo and character of a house that had sunk its roots deep in this soil. Luanda gave herself up to the sheer happiness of the present and stopped fearing that unknown future.

The children wore themselves out tearing round their old haunts and were ready for bed earlier than usual and by a quarter to nine were sound asleep. Luenda slipped an old duffel coat over her bright scarlet jersey and green trews and appeared at the door of the kitchen where Gwillym and Mirabel were both reading, having spurned everything on television.

'I'm going across to Claude's,' she announced, 'I did that errand for him in Arrowtown and I want to see him.'

They looked faintly surprised. 'Take a torch,' advised Gwill, 'some of the pine-roots on the path are a menace.'

She laughed, 'That moon is making it as bright as day. 'Bye!'

Claude heard her coming and came eagerly to the door. 'I was hoping you'd come and kept a good fire on. Sit you down here. It's peaceful tonight with the lads away. Their taste in music is louder than mine and comes through a bit.'

His dog, Tass, the only one of the farm-dogs allowed inside, was stretched out in front of his chair, nose to the fire. Claude bent down, removed a patch of biddi-bids from her coat, threw them in the fire, then said, 'Did you manage it for me?'

'I did. I told Wilkie I wanted a day in Arrowtown by myself, went over on the early bus and back on the late. But I got the flowers in Ludwigtown before I left. They were early violets and primroses, Claude, and the shop put them into one of the little plastic bowls they have, filled with that absorbent oasis stuff that keeps the flowers fresh for ages.

'When I'd put them on Letty's grave a very nice elderly woman came up. She'd been putting flowers on her husband's grave and asked, when she knew I was in the area for only a few days, if I'd like her to pour fresh water in so they'd last even longer. And she said she'd remove them when they did die. She'd only lived in Arrowtown ten years and I didn't say who I was doing it for. That was right, wasn't it, Claude?'

'Aye, Luenda, fine. Letty loved violets and primroses and she died in the spring. I've never let a birthday of hers go by without flowers, and I thought I couldn't manage it this year when Gwill asked me to stay on the place while he was away.'

'I loved doing it, Claude,' she assured him.

'It didn't sadden you too much?'

She looked up at him honestly. 'I couldn't help feeling sad, Claude. I wouldn't have liked myself much if I'd felt any different. And I wept a few tears too. I felt I knew your Letty. Odd how real people you've never met can be,' she mused. 'Sometimes as I take the children through their history, I have this feeling. The early years of Queen Victoria's life, for instance, with the lack of freedom she knew, and all those suspicious uncles ... and the young Elizabeth, with her life constantly menaced, and never able to surrender her life to any man she loved because she dared not trust their motives ... for England's sake.'

Claude nodded, gestured towards his bookshelves. 'I've felt the same so often. Even for Anne of Cleves, who's never been a romantic figure, forced to marry Henry, who despised her. She probably loved Holbein. I'm glad *she* didn't lose her head, but consented to a divorce ... gladdest of all that she was allowed to stay and not be banished, because she so loved England. In fact, people don't have to have been real, for you to feel you've known them. Take Trollope's Phineas Finn ... is it too fanciful to imagine he's sat with me here at this old fireplace?'

'No. My mother was like that. She read to me so much when I was small. She was lonely for years after

my father died. And she and I used to talk as if the
characters were real; you know, Claude, we'd say things
like: "Goodness, she oughtn't to have done that," or: "I
do hope she realises that girl is a liar, out to make
mischief." Sometimes we'd be helpless with laughter, or
cry! It's so good to share books.'

'Aye. That's what I missed most when I lost Letty.
We were looking forward to those sort of hours after
marriage. There was no television then and up here the
reception for radio was very poor. They hadn't the
technique then to cope with these mountains. Her
parents' house was full of books and we had a good
library in the town. We'd each read one, then discuss it
on our long rambles together. We didn't always like the
same books, of course, but that only made it more
interesting. Letty had a most angelic face, but she was a
spirited filly for all that, and even a fair little divil when
she got worked up—she was always championing
someone or something.'

Luenda laughed delightedly. 'Oh, Claude, you've just
brought her to life for me! Till now I thought she was a
little too good to be true. I ought to say *more* to life.
I've felt I knew her from the first mention.'

He laughed. 'She was never that ... too good to be
true. Times we argued fiercely, but that's the way it
should be, you know, Luenda. No one meets up with
the perfect partner. Life would be flat and tame if you
did. I didn't understand Letty to begin with. Sometimes
we even hurt each other. But that never really affected
what we felt for each other under all that. And I'd
rather have had that year of betrothal with Letty than a
lifetime with someone else. She brought a tang to life I
still wouldn't be without.'

Old Claude suddenly laughed at himself. 'I've not
talked to anyone about Letty for so long that now I've
taken the bung out I can't stop! It's your own fault.
You're so like Letitia—the way you walk, the way you
turn your head and your hair swings back. Though hers
turned up at the back. Your voice too, with laughter at
the back of it. You could be the daughter we never had.

Oh, I'm a poetic old fool ... comes of reading too much. Now ... I had some hot cross buns left over from Easter and froze them. The way I like buns is toasted against an open fire on a toasting-fork ... do you? Good, then let's have some. We'll eat, drink, and be merry.'

Into the succeeding silence came that sound so rarely heard here where there were no roads to bring callers ... the sound of knocking at the door. Claude and Luenda looked at each other quite startled, then Claude said, 'It must be Brent.'

It wasn't. It was Gwillym, who said, stepping in, 'Hope I didn't startle you, but Luenda wouldn't take a torch and there's a great bank of cloud come over the moon, so I brought one over and I'll see her home.'

Claude looked knowing. 'Were you thinking I'd let the lassie stumble on her own over those roots? Shame on you! But never mind, clouds or no clouds, it's just the night for roaming in the gloaming.'

If Gwillym wasn't used to that sort of talk from Claude, he hid his surprise very well, Luenda thought. If he'd shown any, Claude would have retired into his shell again. She chalked up a mark in his favour. Claude said, 'You'll have a toasted bun, Gwill?'

He brought out plates, cups, butter, a knife, split the buns, handed them a blackened old fork each. The big log that had blazed so fiercely earlier was now just a cylinder of red-hot ash that would fall apart any moment, but it toasted perfectly. There had been an old iron kettle on the hob all night. The tea was delicious.

The talk didn't turn on farming as Luenda expected. It kept on books, due to Gwillym introducing the subject by drawing out a volume from a nearby shelf and saying he'd like to read it again, Claude nodded approval. 'That's the mark of a good book, wanting to savour it twice. Owning a book is a most satisfying thing—perhaps more necessary in these remote places. Nothing like the backblocks to develop your reading tastes. And nothing so lasting, either. It's hard to feel lonely in a world of books.'

When the toasting was done he built up the fire again from a basket of cones. Gwillym grinned. 'That's a hospitable gesture, Dick. I guess we'll have to see that fire out.'

'Aye. It's been a very pleasant evening all round. You got yourself the right sort of partner, Gwill.'

'Why yes, I think so. She pulls her weight for a start and——' he paused, and surprisingly, it was Claude who prompted him, 'And——'

Gwill considered it, a twinkle in his eye. 'And I simply enjoy having her here. I think that goes for everyone.'

'It does.' Claude turned his lined, weatherbeaten face towards the girl sitting in the big winged chair, her face warm from the fire, and the compliments, 'and especially for me. I was getting far too morose, feeling out of my age group. But she's made me believe that even someone her age can be a real pal to an old codger like me.' They sat in silence for a few moments, then Claude added, 'On your way home, lass, you can tell Gwill what you did for me in Arrowtown. I find it easier now to talk about it, and I'd like to think she wasn't forgotten when my time comes.'

When, suddenly, the glowing red cones disintegrated, she rose, yawned, said, 'If I stay any longer in this heavenly chair, I'll fall asleep!'

Claude got her duffel for her and held it out. While she was fastening the cords across the toggles, he went away and came back with something—a little box.

He put it into her hand. 'It was hers. I want you to have it. I've always worried about what would happen to it when I go. An old goldsmith over at Arrowtown made it for me. We gathered the stones ourselves. They're the stones of this region, from the rivers and waterfalls, agate and carnelian, red jasper, green jasper, rhodonite. Her mother gave it back to me when Letty died. I'd like to see you wearing it at times.'

Gwillym bent down, moved, and patted old Tass to hide his feelings. They said goodnight and moved out into the darkness.

CHAPTER EIGHT

THEY walked in silence till the path veered downhill into the shadow of the pines. Gwillym's hand was under her elbow, his arm warm against her side. He said gently, 'Going to tell me?'

'Yes. Letty was Claude's sweetheart. They were engaged to be married. It was at the end of the Depression. They were saving to buy a cottage in Arrowtown. She got pneumonia, and there were no antibiotics then. Oh, Gwill, doesn't it make you feel like thrusting the life-giving drugs we have today back into those times? But he's marvellous. He'll never forget her, but he doesn't make me feel too sad when he remembers her. He makes me see her as she was—vital, fun-loving, sweet.'

For a moment she didn't think he was going to comment, then he said, '*You've* made me see her too.'

'I have? I'm glad, but I wish you could hear *him* talk about her. I'm just passing it on secondhand; it's not the same.'

Gwillym laughed. 'You underestimate yourself. You forget what Dick said—you're like Letty.'

She was embarrassed. 'Oh, I forgot he said there was a likeness.' Then she thought of something. 'But he didn't say that when you were there. He said it earlier. How——'

He didn't evade it. 'Nobody likes to confess to eavesdropping. But I think you'll understand. Dick's always been so reserved we thought he really did prefer his own company. Wilkie and I are delighted he's opened up. Wilkie says you must be a witch.'

'Oh, now! I think it was the faint resemblance. I had a head start over everyone else. And of course the girls help. They never even notice anyone's shyness, they're so outgoing. But you were saying?'

'So Wilkie and I decided we must leave the two of you alone. But when the moon got obscured I worried about you coming back. I'd just raised my hand to knock when in this still air I distinctly heard Dick say it was good to share books . . . and he mentioned losing someone called Letty. I couldn't break in then, it would have been heartless.

'I felt if old Dick was unburdening himself it wasn't for a third person to intrude. I stayed with my arm upraised to the knocker, didn't know whether to creep away or not, and was just going to when the talk came back to normal . . . toasted buns! I thought it would be okay then. Was it?'

'It was, and it was a compliment to you that Claude went on talking as he did and finished by telling me to let you know what I did for him in Arrowtown. It was to put flowers on the grave in the cemetery, for her birthday. I'm glad he wanted you to know, because he's asked me to do something for him when—if—he dies himself.'

'Yes?'

'Soon after she died and was buried in the family plot, he managed to buy one next to it. He's stipulated in his will that he's to be buried there, but lately he's worked out what he'd like on his grave. It's to mention him as Letty's fiancé. But you should have a copy too, Gwill, because you belong here and I don't.'

He pulled his arm from hers, seized her, swung her round to face him. 'Luenda Morgan! Don't talk such rot. I don't think Megan ever intended your coming here to be as temporary as that. She wouldn't have uprooted your whole lives unless she meant to make it possible for you to stay.' He gave her a little shake, 'You're a wretch! You've asked me to soft-pedal. Personally I like things cut and dried, but I realise this whole situation, the territory, the people, the isolation, is foreign to you, so I've decided to go along with that. But don't keep harping on being here for only a short time or I'll stop soft-pedalling and really crash out a few chords! Now, come on . . .'

She said rather pettishly, 'I like that! It was you who stopped me dead in my tracks.'

He gave a shout of laughter. 'I'm not rushing you inside, you darling nit, I'm rushing you away from the place of argument. With a scene like that below it's a crime to stay in the shadows. Come on, girl, start behaving naturally, forget our first feud. I know I fouled it up. Just remember you're a girl and I'm a man, and there's a moon over Moana-Kotare . . . and we could be the only two in the world. See . . . the moon's come out from the clouds and there's the famous moon-glimmer.'

He was hurrying her towards one of the lower lake-terraces. Luenda caught at his last words. 'The famous moon-glimmer? I haven't heard about this.'

They came to the edge of the terrace and stopped, enchanted. It was so still they could see the faintest reflection of the snow on Serenity in the sable waters, and here and there the sparkle of the stars. The moon was in the perfect postion of dead centre between the dark triangles of Twin Hills all those leagues up-lake, so that its rays slanted with perfect precision to make a glimmering path right across to Ludwigtown.

Gwillym said, 'It's only when it rises early and begins to set that you get it like this. We had a professor of English staying at Twin Hills once, when my mother and sisters and myself were up there for the holidays. He wanted solitude for writing a book. He also wrote poetry. We'd written him off as a dry-as-dust person. But the poem of his we saw, called *Enchantment*, opened our eyes. We were young and callow, with little understanding of people then. But in this poem he listed all the things he'd found enchanting in life, and two of them I remember was "Moon-glimmer on Moana, and the love-light in your eyes." When he'd finished his book, his wife came up from Dunedin. She was years younger than he was, and boy, what a looker! And she adored him. We got so intrigued, we read his book when it came out, and it was so darned interesting it set us reading over again all the classics we'd neglected when we left school.'

Luenda said, in a more amenable tone, 'I like that. But tell me, who do you mean by "we"?'

Gwillym laughed mischievously. 'Ha . . . you thought it was some other female, didn't you? I did say my sisters. But that's good. That's the first spark of interest you've shown in any former love-life I may have had.'

She didn't reply. Oh, yes, she had had an interest all right. A later interest. In Fenella.

The only tribute to the scene below and above them could be paid in silence, so in silence now they watched. Presently Luenda broke it to say, 'Claude spoke of identifying oneself with historical and fictional figures. Now this makes me feel at one with Milton, even if I couldn't express myself as he did, about the moon.'

'Then repeat the bit you're thinking of to me,' commanded Gwillym. 'I think I know it. I learned it at school too.'

She said dreamily:

> *Silence was pleas'd; now glowed the firmament*
> *With living sapphires; Hesperus that led*
> *The starry host, rode brightest, till the moon,*
> *Rising in clouded majesty, at length*
> *Apparent queen . . .'*

She stopped, lifted her chin to look at him in a silent request to finish it. Without hesitation he continued:

> '. . . "unveil'd her peerless light,*
> *And o'er the dark her silver mantle threw." '*

He said, 'Perfect, isn't it, for tonight? Milton in his little world, and us in our little world . . . a different hemisphere, but the same moon.'

Her eyes swept the expanse of the lake, lifted up to the mountains. She said softly, 'But however beautiful his world it couldn't have been *more* beautiful than—than this.'

He corrected her. 'Don't be afraid to say it, girl. Than *our* world.' Then, with a touch of whimsy, he added, 'I hope he didn't see it on his own. I hope he saw it in company with someone as kindred as mine.'

This was heady stuff. Memory swept over her. No wonder she'd never fallen in love with Daryl. He was so nice, but so prosaic—limited, never articulate. Though she supposed that wasn't always a drawback. At that moment Gwillym gave a small laugh and said, 'Oh, look ... we aren't the only ones to appreciate this moon. See, on the jetty ... Josie and Brent.'

They were the only couple within twenty miles, so it had to be them. Two dark figures were silhouetted against that moon-glimmer. As they watched the light between them was blotted out. They had become one.

Luenda said, 'Oh, I'm so glad they still come out and watch the moon together. Josie deserves a husband like that.'

Gwillym promptly drew Luenda under the big macrocarpa that overhung the terrace this end. 'Pity to let them know their idyll had been overlooked, don't you think? They might, if they look up after that kiss, spot us against the light.'

She said, 'They couldn't possibly. *They're* against the light, not *us*. We can walk on.'

He sighed. 'Luenda, for anyone who can recite poetry at the drop of a hat, you really are the unromantic limit! Don't let's waste a moon like that. There mightn't be a lovelier one in a thousand years.'

She said indignantly, 'What a pessimistic outlook, you——' but he silenced her in the only way he knew, and most effectively and long-lasting. When at length he took his mouth from hers, she said breathlessly, 'I said to slow the pace, and you agreed.'

He chuckled. 'You can't make all the rules! You're such a funny girl. A funny, darling girl. You put something into that kiss too ... now come on, didn't you?'

She was silent. He gave her a shake. 'Be honest. What is it? Have you some strange, old-fashioned idea that you like the man to make the running?'

Suddenly she laughed. 'To be really honest, I suppose I do, but also I——' she fumbled for words.

'And also——?'

This time he thought she was laughing at herself, 'I was going to say but also I couldn't *help* responding.'

'Now there's honesty for you,' he admired. 'So let's try it again ... no inhibitions.' Luenda gave herself up to the magic of the night and the moment. Several moments.

Then he said with a hint of laughing ruefulness, 'If Wilkie knew I had you out here in these temperatures, she'd kill me. But I think if we'd not made the most of that moon, we might have regretted it fifty years on, don't you?'

Laughter bubbled up within her. 'You absurd man! What a staggering thought. I'll be seventy-five!'

'And I'll be eighty-three. Isn't it almost impossible to contemplate? I suppose if anyone heard us they'd put it down to the arrogance of youth.'

She nodded. 'Claude's over seventy, a very vigorous seventy, but he said to me once that he feels just the same inside as he did when he was courting Letty. That only the old rheumaticky outside lets him down.'

Gwill said, 'How I wish they'd been able to spend their lives together. But of course that's something none of us can foretell. Nice if they could have been looking back on hours like this, together, instead of just Claude. And other hours, more intimate.'

A tremor passed over Luenda. She felt a tremendous desire to leap into the future, to be able to look back on the here-and-now. Who would stand at her side then? Was there any chance it might be this man? Might they look back on those hours, hours that might have brought children to people their lives, even grand-children ... to know and love Serenity. She knew a passionate longing that it might be so ... but he would have to prove himself trustworthy if that was to come to be.

He felt the tremor and said, 'Luenda, you *are* cold. We must go in. There'll be other moons come summertime.'

The boys came back from their break in the city and

they and Gwillym went up to Hazard Valley and pronounced the dark pool perfectly safe for skating. The children were so excited about getting their skates out. 'This is magnificent,' said Diana, running Gwill to earth in the woolshed. 'We loved our skating-rink in Auckland, but to have a setting like Hazard, the real thing, is a dream come true.'

Gwillym ruffled her hair. 'Once I was anxious about you city youngsters fitting in here, but I could have saved myself a lot of heart-burning. There's something about a high-country sheep station that gets to you, isn't there?'

'There sure is, Gwill.' She looked up at him suddenly, anxiety etching two lines on her broad creamy brow, 'I couldn't bear to leave it now . . . or ever . . . will we be able to stay? I mean, I don't know much about it. About us coming . . . or staying.'

He put an arm about her, hugged her. 'Di, leave it to me. I have definite ideas. Where your sister is, you are, all of you. Well then, *I'm not letting your sister leave here*. I hope you can keep a secret. She's not ready yet to see it my way. I'm only telling you because I don't want you to feel insecure.'

Di's arms shot up round his neck, and she kissed each cheek in her exuberance. 'Oh, Gwill, I do love you! You treat us like grown-ups. How come you feel like that . . . I mean, knowing I want reassuring? Most people in your position would just give me the brush-off.'

He cupped her face in his hands and said, 'Because I was a very insecure, uncertain kid up here. My sisters were training as nurses in Auckland, and in my last year at school I was boarding because Mum had come down here as relieving governess to Twin Hills. Her friend had been in that position and had to go home to nurse her mother. Mum had to, we were running short of money. She married my stepfather, the very best of men, but I hadn't the gumption to see it. I came here resenting everything, hating having to share Mum, longing for the sea, the heat, for my friends, but in six months, the mountains and the lake had got me for keeps. So no worrying, Di, you're here for keeps too.'

Something made him swing round. Luenda was standing in the doorway.

Both Diana and Gwillym looked caught out. Gwillym recovered first and grinned, 'And how long have you been eavesdropping, Miss Morgan? Creeping up on cats' feet!'

'Long enough,' she said drily.

Di was relieved that Gwill didn't look too set back, so she decided on audacity too. 'I rather think, then, dear sister, that you've just been proposed to. How about that?'

Luenda managed to hold her deadpan expression. 'How about that? Well, it's quaint, to say the least. Proposals are usually a matter for two people, not three. So I don't count it.'

Di dimpled. 'Then would you like me to leave?'

'No, stay.' Luenda had decided to keep it light. She waved a hand round the cobwebby shed smelling of dirty daggings and sheep droppings. 'Not my idea of the right setting.'

Di said mournfully to Gwill, 'She's so conventional. She wants moonlight and roses like them all. Better go along with that, Gwill.'

If his cheeks hadn't been grooved in a weatherbeaten sort of way, they'd have dimpled too. 'Have a heart, Di! Roses won't bloom for another six months. She'll have to settle for moonlight alone. But *you* won't be round.'

'I should think not,' said Luenda. 'I'm a bit fed up with you youngsters taking a hand in things. Look at those stupid remarks Davy made when we first got here ... about wolf whistles. Millions I'd had, he said! I can't think what got into him.' She caught a strange look on her sister's face, and her eyes narrowed. 'Come on, Di, what is it? You know something.'

Diana tried to look innocent, but failed. Then she burst out laughing. 'Well, it can't matter now. You see Judy and I started it with the best of intentions.'

Her sister gave a hollow groan, 'I fear the worst. I've

had a long experience of the twins' good intentions.'

Gwill sounded authoritative. 'Give over, Luenda. I'm interested.'

Diana shifted to lean against him affectionately. She said to Luenda directly, 'Well, we thought you were going to take this business of being our guardian far too seriously. We thought you'd broken it off with Daryl because of us. I mean, three children to keep would be a bit putting-off, anyway, so we thought any future suitors would need to worship the ground you trod on.'

Luenda groaned, but gestured for a continuance.

'We thought the outlook pretty grim for you, expecially as it seemed as if Dad had used up so much on travel, so there wasn't much money to come and go on. We thought you would probably feel you had to dedicate your life to us.'

Luenda's lips twitched. 'So . . .?'

Di got a bit stuck. Luenda encouraged her, 'Very dramatic and harrowing, but it wasn't like that. I'd been trying to break with Daryl for ages. We were never in love, just partners. Quite convenient, but the time had come to finish it. I hadn't any time left over. I just wanted to sell the house, repay the mortgages, find somewhere we could afford to live. But go on.'

'Well, we didn't know you didn't care a rap for Daryl, but we thought if he could just let you go, he must think you a ... er ... a dull sort of wench, wedded to duty. To us.'

Luenda clutched her forehead. 'This is getting to sound like one of those Gothic novels I don't like! The heroine sacrificed on the altar of family duty. So you . . .?'

'We couldn't do anything about Daryl, but we thought the very next time a man dawned on your horizon, we'd give you a boost with him.'

'Give me a boost with him? How?' Out of the corner of her eye Luenda could see that Gwillym's hand had come up to hide his mouth.

'That we'd make you sound as if you were really

something with the men. That your—er—past was
positively cluttered with men falling over themselves to
get you.'

Luenda's mouth dropped open. She took a threaten-
ing step towards Diana. Gwillym said, helpless with
laughter and not trying to hide it now, 'Don't, Luenda
. . . it's so long since I've lived with *my* sisters I've
forgotten how crazy girls can be . . . how endearingly
crazy. Whip up your sense of humour, girl. It's just
family life!'

'I don't find anything endearing about it. And you
must have been mad to let Davy in on it, if that's what
made him go on like that.'

Gwill sobered up. 'There's even more to it than that.
I'd better tell you the whole of it, though I found out a
few things myself later, so it didn't matter for long. You
know I warned you off before you came up here, said I
didn't want trouble made among my men, single or
married, and you got as mad as hell? Yes, well, don't go
all hot about that again. It was because of Davy. You
see, he——'

Di got in, 'Please, Gwill, please, Luenda, we *didn't*
rope him in, truly. We went into the old summerhouse,
Luenda, and Davy got up the tree and leaned over near
a pane he'd cracked earlier, and heard the lot. He said it
was the clunkiest thing he'd ever heard, really soppy.
Then he must have decided he'd show us he *could* do it,
even though we'd said he'd be no good at it. But then
when we came up here we just didn't bother. But we didn't
have to.' She waved towards Gwillym, 'It was so
obvious Gwill was falling for you, once he'd got over
the shock of having three females thrust into his
household. A real invasion of his kingdom.'

Luenda gave an exasperated sound, '*Will* you stop
sounding like a Gothic?'

Gwillym said, 'It's time I got hold of the conversation
again myself. Luenda, that first night we met, when I
had the wrong impression of you because of that——'
he encountered a fierce glare from Luenda and in the
nick of time prevented himself from saying 'awful

mannequin parade' and said, 'Well, you know why. No, Di, I will not tell you. Well, you asked Davy to make small talk and when he stopped asking me what I did with my toes in bed ... no, Di, it's quite irrelevant ... he began saying what a knockout of a sister he had. That Auckland was positively littered with swains dying to woo you was the general impression, even if he didn't exactly put it in those words.'

'I shouldn't think he would,' said Luenda, glaring at Gwill in turn.

'He even suggested your boss was madly in love with you ... and as you know, when I called at Ackroyd's to meet you, all I saw was you hugging your boss. It's all right, Di, it was just because his daughter had just had a baby. But it meant that Davy's story fell on fertile ground. So I was a bit hostile ... now, come on, Luenda, laugh! You'll just have to be philosophical and think that with relations like yours who needs enemies.' His dark brows went up in a comical twist, he looked beseeching rather than dictatorial, and Luenda felt her mouth crumbling. The next moment she was helpless. 'My dear, dear family!' she sighed.

'Gosh, am I relieved, or aren't I?' said Diana.

Luenda mopped her streaming eyes and said, 'Right, that's the finish of that episode. A clean slate and all is forgiven. Just keep out of any love-life I may have in the future.'

Diana decided now was the time to beat a retreat, but she paused at the doorway, looked back over her shoulder and said, 'Why the future? Anyway, we don't need to bother any more. You're not going it alone now.'

Luenda said between her teeth. 'I can feel my sense of humour deserting me right now.'

Now Gwillym's tones were dictatorial. 'No! It's not to desert you. The rest is up to me. *I'll* resolve it. Till now you've had the ordering of it. Even two nights ago when there was a superlative moon you declared a slowing-down. Doesn't work, does it, with outspoken children round? Good for them! They go straight to the

crux of the matter, and so will I! But not in this setting.'
His gesture was towards the daggings, the droppings,
the machinery, the cobwebs.

'Besides, we've promised the children their skating
this afternoon. The whole crowd is getting ready.
Forget this for the time being. I'd prefer it to be the
time, the place, *and* the loved one all together, and
above all, no audience. Would you drop my skates into
the Land Rover as you pass it, Luenda? I had to do a
bit of work on them. Tell Wilkie I'll be in sharp at
twelve, will you?'

'I will,' she said. 'I can't tell you how I'm looking
forward to the skating.'

As she went out of the doorway into the bright
winter sunshine his voice followed her. 'Is that all you're
looking forward to?'

And Luenda didn't know. So help her, she just didn't
know.

She had never skated under such perfect natural
conditions before. Hazard Valley was narrow and its
sides thick with trees and sunless, so the ice was thick
and safe and the serrated tops of the pines and larches
made it something out of a Swiss scene.

Mount Serenity, against the deep blue winter sky,
was a white triangle and below them the lake looked as
if someone had dropped a giant opal in blue and green
among the foothills.

Luenda buckled on her skates, looked with loving
eyes at the polished surface. This was her element, her
favourite sport. The girls had wanted her to wear one of
her special outfits, but she'd refused. 'I just want to
enjoy myself, not rub it in that I'm an expert.'

Di had said, 'She no longer wants to score off Gwill,
Judy. No need to.'

A look from Luenda had quenched her. Judith
sounded scathing. 'As if I didn't know! We never saw
Luenda like this with Daryl.'

Luenda said quietly, 'I don't want to hear any more
about this, girls. I'd like you to respect my privacy.

You've had your fun. I'm trying to sort my feelings out. How about leaving me alone?'

Two sober faces looked back at her. Though the twins were by no means identical, at times their thoughts and moods seemed one. They nodded and said in duet, 'Okay, Luenda. It's your life.'

Their mature response lifted her heart and spirit. She said, 'Thanks, girls. Now I feel better—not harried or hurried. Let's go.'

Now they were on the ice. Was there ever a more glorious feeling? As if one's very spirit had wings. The keen air, the piney resinous tang from the pines, the sound of larks so high in the sky they were unseen, the sunlight on the ebony flanks of the Black Galloway cattle up in a gully to the right of Hazard.

When they had limbered up Judith said, 'Why don't you and Gwill take it together, Luenda. He's pretty good, isn't he?'

'He certainly is. Can you follow with me, Gwill, holding hands?' Her tone was matter-of-fact.

'Do a few turns and figures by yourself first, to give me the idea.'

She set off, keeping it simple, the exhilaration of it sending carnation-bright colour into her cheeks and a svelte grace to her body. It did something for her . . . she'd been the new chum up here for so long, awkward and ignorant. She'd put her foot in it time and again— or rather her tongue—on farm matters.

She came back to the edge, Josie and Mirabel were entranced. But it was the delight in Gwillym's eyes that pleased her most. He said, 'I'm probably about to make a fool of myself, but I'll give it a go.'

'You're so proficient on the plain stuff, you'll make it, I know,' she said, held out her hands and away they went, Gwill gaining more confidence every moment. She said, as the air rushed by them, 'I can tell you'd be a wonderful dancer.'

'I can get by. I suppose I have a sense of rhythm, and after all, most winters we rarely miss a dance in Ludwigtown.'

A new sensation to Luenda hit her amidships, a stupid, unreasoning jealousy of all the girls he'd held close when dancing. She made a slight faltering, Gwillym's hands tightened and he swept her on, then curved round to come back and do it again. Their eyes met. 'Thank you,' she said. 'What an anticlimax if I'd been the one to make a fool of myself.'

'You lost your concentration for a moment, that's all. It can happen to anyone. I suppose you realise that once the Ludwig Skating Centre finds out about you, you'll be in great demand? Will you go along with that? Become one of the community? Do a bit of coaching? It'd mean a lot to them.'

'I guess I will. But I don't want to enter for any championships. I haven't skated since Mother was ill. I would like to do it for sheer delight.'

'I want to see you about that—I mean about all you went through before you came here. What you meant about those mortgages. Tonight, after tea, I've decided on.'

They came back to the sound of applause and laughter. The three single men were raring to have a turn with her. They weren't as proficient as Gwill, but they enjoyed it, spills and all, but Luenda had been watching Claude on his solitary turns and knew what she wanted; she held out her hands to him.

As they swept away he said, 'Thank you, lass. I've not skated double since Letty went—I never wanted to. Till I saw you go down the ice with Gwillym.'

After a few moments she said, 'Claude, you've certainly not lost the art.'

'I suppose we never lose what we learn when we're young. But unfortunately, some lessons come too late.'

They swirled and swooped, then she said, 'Claude, do you mean something to do with Letty? But there was no remorse there, was there? A tragic loss, but no one's fault.'

The kind dark eyes looked into hers, his grip on her hands tightened. 'We could have been married months earlier. Who knows, she might never have contracted pneumonia then. But apart from that, I'd have given her the fulfilment she was eager for ... marriage, a home of her own. But her people were better off than I was and I had far too much silly pride.

'I set my heart on having a good bank balance so I could put a good deposit down on the cottage we hoped for, to be able to furnish it as I wanted it, up to her parents' standards. She said she wanted to share the struggle, didn't mind scrimping and scraping, as long as we were together, that it would be fun. I denied her that, Luenda.'

He guided her expertly to the far edge of the pond. 'I'll say this without having to keep my mind on my feet ... and your feet ... I've an idea you and Gwill got off to a bad start. He rang Wilkie from California, you know, and was anything but pleased. Happen he let a bit of that show in Auckland. Sometimes to know all is to understand all. He was pretty angry still with a girl up here who was obviously on the make. She was fair poisonous, that one. She'd have had him out of here before all the bride-cake was eaten if he hadn't seen through her. So he was suspicious of women's motives. But he's a changed man since you came here.'

He frowned. 'I'm not one for meddling, but go easy, lass. You've told me how you were left when your stepfather died. You said Josie was the only other one you'd told. I think that because you were left with so little, you're afraid to give in to your feelings for Gwill in case he thinks you're looking on him as a financial solution. Don't let pride stand in your way. A lass like you, who can adapt to this sort of life in the way you have, is nothing but an acquisition to the place, and a fitting partner for him. On these only-access-by-water stations, a man needs a wife like you. Wilkie can't stay here for ever. And he'd never look on the children as a liability. You can see how he loves them. He was such a lonely little codger when he first came up here. It'd be stupid to let the fact that your financial situations aren't equal keep you apart. Life's too short. You're twenty-five, he's over thirty. The years have a habit of robbing us. Think on that, lass. Now an old man will shut up. One more long swoop up to them, and back to the homestead. The shadows are lengthening.'

All through the laughing ride back in the Land Rover and the truck, then through the meal the others did such justice to, Luenda's thoughts were chaotic. Till now old Claude had been almost a recluse, so there'd probably been no real clarification of the situation regarding the disposal of the estate, as far as he was concerned. Therefore, when the astute old man had sensed her reluctance, he'd thought it was her pride in the way. He probably thought Megan had offered them a year up here with a view to matchmaking.

Whereas she herself was holding back because she'd been forewarned that Gwill, despite the admirable virtues she'd found out for herself, was land-hungry. That if an unknown girl was probably having half the estate dropped in her lap, what better than marriage? She'd adapted to the life, was a fair cook ... was beginning to be useful outside. A good blueprint.

Like a flash she remembered the caresses of the other night, the depth of their conversation, the quoting of poetry. She couldn't, honestly, equate that with a cold-blooded sense of her suitability. Had it meant as much to Gwillym as to her? Or was he persuading himself it did? Was there any equality in their loving? Had he felt something stronger, more vital, for that beautiful girl who had sunk her pride to come to Luenda in Auckland? And what did Claude really know about it, and her?

Yet all Luenda wanted was to live the rest of her life here, with Gwillym. So often love between two people wasn't quite equal. People were rarely geared the same, but as the years went by they grew together. It balanced out. They became one.

Some women, for instance, came to marriage unawakened, unaware of the depth of passion of which they were capable, and found a new world of delight. Luenda's mother had talked deeply with her daughter in those weeks when she knew she must leave three girls to find their way through life. Some women thought they knew all the answers, but found in one man heights not dreamed of before. Some men, too, had thought of love as only part of the natural order of things, and found in the personality of someone who shared their waking and sleeping hours undreamed-of joys, and a rich sharing of interests that enhanced their whole existence.

But there was also the darker side, the doubts and fears. If one started off with quite a few of those, what then, Luenda?

Wilkie brought her out of her reverie. 'I just can't get over it. Luenda's just pecked at her food, and look what the others have eaten. I've never known skating fail to make people ravenous. Do you feel well, Luenda? You look to me as if you're either off-colour, or tired out, or worried about something. Is there anything on your mind, dear?'

She saw Gwillym look at her quizzically, and was furious with herself when she felt warmth in her cheeks. Wilkie persisted, 'But what could it be? We've had no mail for three days, so no bad news. What is it, love?'

Gwill saved her, 'Wilkie, that presupposes bad news comes only from outside, that Serenity is a carefree, tax-free haven. That nothing here could possibly worry our Luenda. And *nothing need.*'

Luenda said hurriedly, 'Will someone please change the subject? I feel like a worm under a microscope! I'm perfectly all right.'

'Of course she is,' said Diana complacently.

CHAPTER NINE

LUENDA thought that could be the end of it. Vain hope! Diana beamed on Gwill in the most conspiratorial manner. 'Not to worry about her, Gwill. It's probably only emotional. Luenda said once that she'd rather things happened, even if they weren't always nice, than nothing happened. Our mum said to watch a statement like that, it was—er—second cousin to enjoying being miserable.'

Luenda protested, 'Stop dissecting me! Gwill said this morning I didn't need enemies with relations like mine, and he never spoke a truer word. I did ask for a change of subject.'

Davy obliged. 'It's boring, anyway. Look what I found on the edge of the pond,' and out of a deep pocket he fished a treasure and laid it tenderly on his table-mat. The girls shrieked. It was the skeleton of a tiny lizard.

'Gosh, listen to them, will you! It's been dead for ages. No smell, and clean as a whistle, you clunky things.'

Gwill pushed his chair back, came quickly to Davy and said, 'Davy, that's really a find. How on earth did you manage to keep it in your pocket without it falling to pieces? That's a fossil. It's been in limestone.' He put a finger against it and it came away all powdery. 'This must go in the glass case in the schoolroom and we'll make a report on it to the Archaeological Society. It must have been washed down in a chunk of limestone and perhaps cast up when the pond was flooded. Did you find it on the edge this side?'

Luenda was grateful for the lizard. But why had she supposed it would head Di off? That one took a drink of lemonade and said, 'Anyway, it wasn't said about me. It was about Davy. About not needing enemies.'

Davy left his rapt adoration of the skeleton and said, 'What do you mean? I'm not Luenda's enemy—I'm her brother and her best friend. I don't upset her the way you do. Girls are always flying into tizzies. And about the most ridic'l'us things. Like when *can* they wear eyeshadow and nail polish and——'

Di cut in, 'It was *so* you! And your mad scheme for boosting Luenda's stock. All that rot you told Gwill in Auckland . . . about Daryl and her boss and——'

Davy turned purple. 'I'd never have thought of it if it hadn't been for you two hatching the thing up, and lemme tell you——'

Gwill's voice brought him to a complete halt. 'This is *quite* enough! I will *not* have you embarrassing your sister like this. It was only a jest about the enemies, Davy, and Di, may I remind you that even as a jest it was meant to be kept quiet. Now, you can start washing the dishes. By hand, not in the washer. No, Judith, you aren't to dry, and you aren't to question her.

'You can turn up the heat in all the bedrooms—it's going to be a freezing night. And when you've done that feed the cats and Griff, and cut up enough meat for them for the morning and put it in the safe. Davy, take that lizard very carefully to the schoolroom, then you're to scrape all the gumboots on the back porch, on newspaper, before the mud hardens too much. Wilkie, put your feet up and listen to the news. What are you giggling for, woman? It's time I began to be head of this house. I'm sure I come off a long line of patriarchs, only I'm a late starter. Luenda and I have some pretty solid items of business to discuss in my sitting-room. *What* did you say, Di?'

She said hurriedly, removing plates with great diligence, 'It—it wasn't really meant for general hearing.'

Davy, still enraged at being blamed for what he did in Auckland, said, 'She said: "Is that what you call it? Business?" '

Gwillym's tone brooked no more asides. 'I'd better cross the t's and dot the i's for you, then you'll know it's business. You started this off when you mentioned this morning about money being tight when you lost your father. Luenda and I have never had a really frank talk about your circumstances, and as we're partners, it needs to be done. If that isn't business, what is? And let me tell you we want no interruptions. Come on, Luenda.'

She found herself being swept out. He didn't pause till they reached the landing, then he looked down on her. 'I know those trews and that jersey are warm, but I do like women in dresses at night.'

She said, 'I do myself as a rule, but tonight I——' He tried to prompt her. 'No, I'm usually in trouble, Gwill, for speaking without thinking. On the rare occasions I have second thoughts, people would be wise not to ask what I'd been going to say.' Her dimples flashed out and a flake of colour stained her cheeks.

'That's better,' he said. 'When you wouldn't eat and you were so quiet I thought we'd tired you to death. I don't want you tired tonight.'

'Why not tonight?' Oh dear, she shouldn't have asked that. It was as bad as what she'd choked back when she'd nearly said, 'I didn't want it to look as if I was dressing up for a special occasion.'

His eyes showed a flicker of amusement. 'Because no one feels like talking business if they're tired,' he said gravely. 'Wear something that suits Letty's necklace.'

What could that have to do with business? She had a quick shower. She brushed her streaky gold hair till it shone like a stubble field in sunlight, the fringe slanting above her brows, the sides swirling back to show her tiny ears. She knew what would suit Letty's necklace best. And she was lucky to have earrings that would go with it beautifully.

She took out a soft woollen georgette dress, a fabric come back into favour and enhanced by a little polyester, in a muted gold. It had a deep cowled neckline and under those soft folds the bodice was very fitting. The skirt was slightly gored, all simplicity and elegance.

She fastened the necklace, and as she felt its stones against her flesh, magic touched her. Here was romance, and romance gilded life, as Mother used to say. Suddenly she felt very near her mother. Above the rich polished browns and topazes, reds and greens of the stones of riverbed and lake, her brown eyes glowed, glad that Gwillym couldn't help but admire her in this. She lifted her mother's earrings out and fastened them in. Her own father had given them to her mother for a birthday. They were single topazes, to fit against her lobes, and half-inch golden chains swung from them.

She picked up a bottle of yellow kowhai perfume from her dressing-table, touched her wrists with it and the hollow in her throat. That too belonged to this area. In spring those *kowhais* down by the lake would hang golden tassels above it, and bellbirds and tuis would sip their nectar. Oh, what a goose she was! Business, he'd said.

And business it was, but first he rose from his chair by the fire, came to her, took her hands, held her off and surveyed her, then said, 'Very nice. My stepfather always liked Mother to change, no matter what she wore if she was helping at the dip during the day. We lived in the Hemmingways' house, you know.'

He led her across to the other chair and said, 'Now come clean, Luenda. Twice or more something's been said about how you were left, and I'd like to be put in the picture. What's wrong about telling me? I asked Claude if he knew, and he said to ask.'

Luenda swallowed, but knew she must be truthful. 'I didn't want to confess to you at our unfortunate first meeting just how bad our financial position was in. I thought you'd think I played on Megan's sympathy, but I didn't. She was merely sorry for me because we'd lost our mother, then when she was in the States she heard about Dad's death. At first you and I didn't seem kindred spirits. We know now you had a false idea of me, and no wonder!' A little smile touched her lips. 'So I didn't want to talk about Dad. What happened to him after Mother died makes him seem weak. And he wasn't—till then. I loved him dearly. He made such a happy home for us—never treated me any differently from his own daughters and son. In fact we were very close. But he suffered a complete change of personality after Mum died. He just went to pieces. Can you understand that, Gwillym?'

'Yes. Oddly enough it happened, in a minor way, I suppose, to Megan, after she lost Evan. She'd never handled any finance till then, and she got fascinated by it, began playing the Stock Exchange. She made a couple of lucky strikes and got carried away. My father and Mr Stillman had to come to the rescue. Dad was still manager here then and the idea was I should take over. Her losses gave her a scare, and she pulled in her horns. Does that make it easier to tell me about your stepfather? I know now there was still a mortgage on the house.'

'It was worse than that,' said Luenda. 'He started to travel—Australia first, Singapore, Hong Kong, then he took expensive cruises. Then a tour of America, and he went across to Europe. We didn't worry at first, we thought he'd get his grief out of his system. We thought his business must be doing excellently well. It was looked after for him by reliable men. They did their best when they found out what he'd done.

'He got carried away at the gaming tables. He came home, then went off, as we thought, for another tour of the States. He spent the whole time at Las Vegas—couldn't tear himself away from the tables. He'd mortgaged everything up to the hilt, borrowed against his insurances, the lot. He thought, I suppose, that some time he'd recoup the lot and quit. I'm not excusing him, he should never have played ducks and drakes with the children's future, but I couldn't set that weakness he developed, against the rest of his life which had been one of kindness and integrity. So I hated telling anyone what had happened. When he finally lost a terrible amount, he had a heart attack, in the casino. There wasn't even enough left to buy us a small flat. We couldn't afford to pay rates and mortgage repayments to stay where we were, not just out of my wage and the child allowance. So when this came it was like a miracle.'

Gwillym came across to her, knelt beside her chair and took her hand. 'Then I came along, blazing mad about the kind of girl I *thought* you were, and shivered that miracle into splinters for you, clod that I am!'

She turned against the wing of the chair. It brought her face on a level with his. She put a finger against his lips in reproof. 'No, Gwill, don't whip yourself. It was natural. Only I just had to take that windfall—a whole year without expenses! I had to sink my pride and accept.'

He took the hand and rubbed his face against it. The small gesture of sympathy and understanding moved Luenda greatly. How could she have entertained doubts of this man?

She thought of something. 'You're taking what I say as absolutely true, Gwill. Aren't you going to ask how Megan found out we were in need?'

'No, I'm not. I'll take it on trust. She did, somehow. And just as well, otherwise we might never have met.'

'But I'm going to make sure you do know, or there'll come a time when you might wonder. Tell me, Gwill, when you flew over for Megan's funeral, did someone called Beverley Menton fly from Canada for it? A close friend of Gillian's, though nearly twenty years younger.'

He took his time replying to that. Then slowly, he said, 'Why are you asking that, Luenda? What do you know? Do you know Beverley? But how?'

She answered carefully. 'She's my aunt—my own father's adopted sister. She's been away from New Zealand a long time, but I always loved her. We still write. But I didn't know of the connection with Megan till Megan looked me up.'

He said, 'Well then, it's all right for me to say I know that she's Gillian's daughter. Did your grandparents adopt her? And is this the favour Megan was repaying?'

She smiled into his eyes. 'That was it. You can see

why I didn't want to say—it wasn't my secret. Who told you, Gwill?'

'Gillian did. When Beverley married and went to Canada, Gillian told her husband about it. He was very understanding, had been through the war himself. It's a very happy relationship. I suppose Beverley thought it was better not to tell you. I wish I'd been told a bit more. It might have saved me hurting you so much, crass fool that I was.'

'My pride was responsible for some of that, so forget it. Besides, Gwill, you've cancelled out a lot by being so marvellous with my sisters and brother in spite of distrusting me. I don't blame you for thinking how unsuitable I'd be for the life up here, when you saw me gliding towards you in that awful dress, and kissing my boss . . . and that wretched Davy making me out a . . . a *femme fatale*!'

She was swept with laughter, wonderful, irresistible healing laughter. Gwillym pulled her to her feet, laughing with her, holding her by the elbows. 'Oh, Luenda, we shall deal famously together. Dad always said, "Get yourself a wife with a sense of humour, my boy, you can't beat it." He's going to love you!'

He stopped, looked comically dismayed, said, 'Now look what you've made me do, with being so sweet! You've jumped the gun. Oh, Luenda, Luenda, Di said you wanted moonlight and roses, I said I wanted the time and the place and *the loved one* all together . . . and though I couldn't wait for roses to bud, I thought another night of lake and moon-glimmer might do instead, and that blasted fog came up tonight. But I can't help it now . . .' his hands left her elbows and slid down to grasp her fingers, 'Luenda, you *know* I love you, I *can't* mark time any more . . . promise to marry me, girl? Is this too ordinary a setting?' His hand waved at the shabby sitting-room.

Luenda, as in a dream, looked about her . . . the firelight in dancing reflections on the polished panelling, the dual picture of the first Evan and Myfanwy above the mantelpiece, the old Welsh dresser where Gwill had

books stacked, then her eyes came back to the eyes of
the man holding her and she said softly, 'It *is* the time
and the place, Gwill . . . I wouldn't have it any other.
Or wait any longer. Moonlight and roses can't compare
with this!'

She felt an exultant tremor go through him. He said,
'You didn't finish that quotation. I'm waiting for it.'

She laughed, a low happy sound. '*And the loved one.*
Yes, you are that, Gwillym. Only I was so afraid you
were acting too quickly, that you might regret it, I——'

But anything else was lost in the fervour of his
embrace. She was caught to him in a hold like a vice,
yet his kiss was tenderly passionate, giving as well as
taking. This time she clung to him in true surrender, all
doubts swept away.

When at last they drew apart simply because they
needed to breathe, he said, 'God bless old Dick . . . I'll
even call him Claude if you like . . . and his Letty. I
reckon they softened you up. It seems incredible but true.
Luenda, you can't do less than ask him to give you away.'

Her eyes widened, 'Gwill, don't go so fast! You've
only just proposed!'

'What's the point in waiting? Don't forget we're
living in the same house. What a strain that'll be if you
want a long engagement.'

She chuckled, 'I didn't mean a long engagement,
darling, but truly, you don't start planning the
ceremony immediately.'

He was irrepressible. 'I've been thinking of it for ages
. . . well, it seems ages. When I told you about Mum
and Dad being married in the Chapel-on-the-lake, I
wanted to say to you, "We'll be married there." But
right now, I'll leave it alone, we have better things to
do. Let's sit by the fire and just talk about ourselves . . .
and perhaps *not* talk!'

As he led her across to it, she said, 'I never did
explain how Megan must have got to know about our
changed circumstances.'

'Does it matter?'

'It does. Beverley must have told her. I let her know

about Dad and Las Vegas, of course. I think Megan
must have wanted to meet Beverley, her until-then-
unknown niece, when she went across.'

He nodded. 'And now, my sweet, this time is to be
ours alone.'

That hour was so magic that Luenda pushed down
into the limbo of all things best forgotten the memory
of the day Fenella had come to see her. With it also, she
discarded the idea she had implanted, that Gwillym was
land-hungry, that he might consider a partner foisted
upon him, as a possible bride bringing him the other
half. It was unlikely Megan would do anything for her
on so large a scale.

Besides, ever since Luenda had found out Fenella was
completely wrong about Wilkie being prejudiced about
Australians, she'd wondered if anything she'd told her
could have been true. And Claude had spoken of some
girl who'd been on the make. Luenda consigned these
thoughts to the deeps. Nothing must spoil this, the
happiest night of her life . . . to date.

Presently, reluctantly, Gwillym stirred, lifted her chin
from his chest with one finger under it, kissed her
lightly this time and said, 'Out of sheer consideration
for the others we ought to go down to tell them.
Otherwise Wilkie will have them off to bed. Come on,
love.'

Luenda uncurled herself and stood up, tall, willowy,
though not as tall as he. 'Supple as a willow-wand,' he
told her, 'though more curved!' Then, 'We won't really
need to say a word. We'll go in hand in hand, but apart
from that, your eyes are shining and you've a lovely
colour. Come on.'

As they went along the upstairs passage he stopped at
a door. 'This is sheer sentiment, but there's a call I want
to pay first.'

His hand found the knob of the master bedroom
door. He flung it open, pressed the switch down. That
switch controlled two sets of wall-lights, dim enough to
be romantically reminiscent of the candleglow of
pioneer days. They didn't speak for a moment or two.

Words weren't necessary in that closeness of thought, their awareness of the promise this room held of greater fulfilments to come.

That old sturdy wooden bedstead had come out from Wales with Evan and Myfanwy Richards and had come up here on a bullock cart and across lake by barge. The white knitted quilt had been theirs. It had been modernised by some later bride with lavender satin spread beneath its openwork. The small paned windows were frosted over with ice-ferns tonight, but they knew that through all the years to come they would watch countless dawns there, breaking over the lake.

Gwillym walked her round the far side of the bed, opened the door into the little room. They looked at the teddy-bear sitting on the cot, shabby, with nibbled ears, and laughed.

He said, 'Why do I feel as if these ancestors are mine? As if they'll be forebears of our children? It's so strong.'

Her smile deepened. 'Not all strong ties are those of blood. Ties between husband and wife are strongest of all. So are the ones that bind you to this station, and it's right they should. The third Evan, and Megan, had no family to leave this to. It's a trust, isn't it? You've so identified with it, it belongs to you.' She reached up and kissed him.

He said, 'I'm glad Rosamond MacQueen didn't call her little daughter Serena. I think we're entitled to that, aren't we? Was that what you thought that day? Do admit it, I'd like to think you did.'

'I did. But felt I shouldn't have had thoughts like that. I didn't know you well enough then.'

'Were you trying to stop falling headlong in love, too?'

'Must have been. I didn't trust my instincts. I thought it was too soon.'

He turned to her. 'But not now? No doubts left? No, you don't need to answer that. I know it seems quick, but it hasn't been like an ordinary case. We were thrust into life on an isolated sheep-run, with never a neighbour, never a road, only a tourist launch now and

again. So we've really got to know each other. Very few
other folk to clutter up our lives and complicate things.
Our future seems set fair.' He paused, then, reflectively,
'Yes . . . Serena . . . I'd like a daughter called after our
mountain.'

They were suddenly swept with the absurdity of it.
'Oh, dear, we've just got engaged,' said Luenda, 'and
we're already deciding on names for our offspring. How
ridiculous . . . but I would like one of the boys to be
Evan.'

They clung together, laughing helplessly.
'Downstairs,' said Gwillym. They came in as they
planned, hand-in-hand, but were greeted by four backs,
sunk deep in chairs, watching TV. Before anyone
turned, the phone rang. Gwillym muttered, 'Of all
moments!' and picked it up. Music signalled the end of
a programme, and Wilkie switched off to save Gwillym
going into the hall to the extension.

Over the instrument Gwill raised his brows comically
in exasperation, at Luenda, then next moment his voice
warmed. 'Marie? Yes, quite free this weekend. What did
you say? An ice-spree to mark the end of the school
holidays . . . yes, ours is in perfect condition too. But of
course yours is so much larger. That'd be marvellous, a
real old-timer. Marie, did you know Luenda is a
topnotch skater? I reckon I could persuade her to do
some exhibition stuff. How about that? What did you
say? My glory, you're having a huge crowd if you're
going to invite all those. Yes, we'll bring bedrolls and
our own food. And we'll bring stuff for the barbecue.
We've only to raid our deep-freeze, and I reckon the
MacQueens and the MacCorquodales will do the same.

'Marie, you couldn't have arranged this at a better
time,' he went on. 'We've a reason to celebrate. Make it
an engagement party . . . Luenda and I have just got
ourselves engaged. Oh, Marie, do excuse those shrieks
in the background . . . Luenda and I had just come in to
tell the family and before we could, you rang. Now
they're hurling themselves at us! Look, I'll ring you
back in a few moments when the shouting and tumult

dies. Oh, thanks, Marie ... yes, it's true what you've heard, Luenda *is* the girl for the lake. 'Bye for now!'

The next moment he was gazing at Wilkie and saying: 'What are you *crying* for?' Mirabel was mopping her eyes impatiently, and she said, 'I'm too happy not to cry. Oh, Gwill, it's so perfect! And wouldn't Megan be happy? Oh, I'm sure she'll know. It looks to me as if she planned it.'

Davy, somewhat pushed to the background managed to say, 'Anybody with half an eye could see what was going to happen.' He grinned. 'Perhaps I didn't make such a bluey after all when I boosted her!'

'Listen to that!' said Judy disgustedly. 'Our idea and he cops the credit!'

Diana said impishly, 'I know the roses were out of season, dear brother-in-law-to-be, but it looks as if you dispensed with the moonlight too.'

'Moonlight,' said Gwill, 'wasn't essential. Only Luenda was!'

CHAPTER TEN

MORNING brought an enchantment all its own. Not only did Luenda wake to the glorious realisation that all was well with her world, that Gwillym loved her, that the children's future was assured, but the world outside was a fairy-tale one.

She was wakened by a knock at her door and voices clamouring for her to get up, and she could distinguish Gwill's deep voice above all the rest. 'Come on out, Luenda ... we want to show you something you've never seen before!'

She leapt out, snatched a long gown, wrapped it round her and, not waiting to tie it, reached the door. Wilkie had got to the group by then too, and Luenda heard from the babble, 'It's a hoar-frost, it's like seeing Christmas trees in crystal!'

Gwillym was laughing. Above Davy's black head, he bent over and kissed Luenda lightly. 'What a family! But you must come. One's first sight of a real hoar-frost is really something. That fog froze. It's perfect. Tie that round you, love, because we'll have to slide the windows up, they're frosted right over.'

What a magic, incredible world! The larches with their curved branches indeed glittered as if they'd been dipped in glass, every drop from the fog had hung and crystallised. The macrocarpa hedges so solidly sheltering were spangled with frost diamonds, and cobwebs were miracles of silver filigree. The barbed wire fences, so ugly in themselves, were diamanté ribbons, interspersed with stars. The pines had a coating of powder, every ridge of the outhouses was lined with a crusting of frozen particles. Down at the lake-edge the water-birds were protesting at this change in their environment. One rose with a raucous cry and swept up in flight to the bare branches of the liquid-amber and alighted. In the still austere air they heard a tinkle as transparent splinters of ice fell from the twigs. 'In all the years I've spent up here,' said Gwillym, 'I've never heard or seen that happen before. Judith, what a good job you've shut the poultry in and that you've got pine-needles all over the floor. This won't last, and it means we've a lot to do ... it's beautiful, dangerous, and we don't want any broken limbs to mar this weekend, so you must work under instructions. There'll be a lot of feeding-out, but it's got to be done under strict precautions.'

Just as well the weekend was two days off. The sun came out brilliantly, thawing the exquisite traceries very quickly, and it left the next day fairly free for Luenda and Wilkie to do a huge baking, ably assisted by Diana and Judy, who chopped nuts, iced cakes, filled kiss-cakes and enjoyed themselves.

The Hemmingways weren't coming, having just got back from a few days in Dunedin, but Gwillym insisted Dick Turpin came. 'There was a special invitation for you,' he told him. 'Old Mac Billington's visiting Twin Hills and specially asked for you, Marie said. I believe you were at school together. Besides, it's nice for Luenda to have you. Don't forget you're standing in for her father at the wedding. It's to be in July, by the way, midwinter. You did a lot towards making this match, Claude, you created the right atmosphere. And you're a darned good skater, remember.'

Friday was perfect, the air keen, but the sky cloudless, a deep winter-blue, with the mountains glittering white against it. Luenda had met Marie and Geoff Campion only briefly, when they were in Ludwig-town the other week, but felt she'd known them for years.

It was wonderful to find Dr Justin and Barbara MacCormack among the guests. They'd come up for the last weekend of the holidays, Marie had heard of it, and had invited them specially for Luenda's sake. 'I felt you ought to have someone from your former life here, though if you're joining the over-lake community, you aren't a stranger. I've heard from Wilkie, per telephone, how you've fitted in.'

Luenda was enchanted to meet Rosamond MacQueen, the girl from Southampton, and met Gwillym's eyes in secret mirth as she picked up her baby daughter ... and was told she'd been called Margot Louise after Matthieu's great-grandmother, and Rosamond's grandmother.

Just as well Twin Hills was the largest homestead on the lake. The old pioneer house joined the new one, was preserved as a showplace of other days, and was a great tourist attraction. But this weekend it was pressed into service to accommodate the forty-odd guests assembled. Most had brought bedrolls that were simply placed on the old bedsteads and couches and saved huge washings of linen later for the Campions. Everyone had brought provisions, and all pitched in to serve the meals. The bay below the house was thick with launches.

They made it an engagement supper that night. Luenda had thought she would be celebrating it with her hand innocent of an engagement ring, but she was very mistaken. The Ludwigtown jeweller and his wife were there, and after tea Luenda was drawn into Geoffrey's sanctum by Gwillym, and there was the jeweller with some shallow boxes. 'Any preference, Luenda?'

'Have you, Gwill? It should be a dual choice.'

He grinned, 'I ought to say "after you," but I'd love to see you wearing an emerald. I love you in green.'

'That's a good choice. It's my birthday next week, so the emerald is my birthstone.'

'Is it really?'

The jeweller boggled. 'Mean to say you're engaged to her and you didn't know when her birthday was? Gwill, you've had a lucky escape. Women set great store by anniversaries. You'd better buy her a pendant to match.'

'Oh, the children would have told me,' Gwillym assured him.

'Children? Hers?'

Luenda laughed. 'Sort of. My half-sisters and a half-brother. Isn't he the brave one? Think what he's taking on!'

Gwill said quickly, 'Not a millstone, Luenda, more of a bonus. I've not been a member of a family for so long I think it's great.' He grinned at the jeweller. 'Harry, I've only known Luenda two months. No, three. I've a lot more than birthdays to find out.'

The ring they chose fitted perfectly—an emerald with a circle of diamonds. A heavy ring, which suited her lean strong fingers beautifully. 'And we'll choose the wedding ring right now. We live too far for frequent shopping sprees. Are you with me, Luenda, if I say a broad, heavy gold one, enduring?'

Harry fossicked. 'There's one here made from gold from this area. Still a bit of mining and prospecting goes on. This came from Skipper's Canyon not long ago. I had a yen to have a ring of local gold in case I ever came across someone sentimental enough to want one.'

It needed tightening a little. She had an odd feeling as Gwill said. 'I'll pick it up next time I'm over. The wedding's the month after next.'

Harry grinned. 'Making sure of her, are you?'

Gwillym nodded. 'Can't be too careful. Look what happened to that fellow writing up the history of Twin Hills. A bad business that, thought I believe it's patched up again.'

Harry said, 'I heard it was. Thank goodness. You'd never have believed that girl could have been such a bitch, could you? She looked like something out of a Greek myth. Though come to think of it, some of them were real trouble-makers. I heard that author bloke marched his girl across to Sydney ... well, flew her there ... and confronted t'other one and made her admit he'd never as much as made a pass at her. Beats me. Seems she liked to make mischief for the sheer joy of it.'

'That about fits the bill, or so Marie said. They thought they wouldn't risk bringing another governess here. But they feel Alison and Rory are too young to go away from home and Marie's too busy for supervision of lessons. But they've had a real stroke of luck. They're getting their old governess back. She had to go away to housekeep for her father, but he's getting married again. She's dying to get back. She's due next week.'

They weren't looking at Luenda. Just as well. A variety of expressions were chasing across her face—suspicion, wonder, enlightenment, hope. Harry snapped his cases shut, said, 'You'll want privacy to put that on, so I'm off. I'd advise you, with a crowd like this, to turn that key.'

Gwill did, then came back to her, ring in hand. She said, 'Oh, Gwill, I must ask you . . . oh, please don't be vexed about it . . . me accepting it as gospel, but tell me, please, if . . .'

He held up a hand, 'My dear love, it sounds controversial, and nothing of that nature is going to mar this moment. This is the biggest in our lives till now. Hold out your hand, sweetheart.' ·

She held it out. His eyes held hers, and he said, 'I hope this means all happiness for us both, but other things too. I want there to be between us an absolute trust, always. Harry reminding me of what Fenella Newbolt did to an engaged couple made me think of this. We don't know what's ahead of us in the years to come, what cross-currents could affect our lives, and I've an idea that where you're concerned, I could be a pretty jealous chap, given cause. But let's make a pact to trust each other, and if ever anything threatens our relationship, let's ask straight out and clear it up.'

He couldn't read her expression, but the well-curved lips began to go up at the corners. 'I couldn't agree more. So, Gwill, I'm not putting you on the spot. As soon as Harry mentioned that governess, I realised that what Fenella Newbolt told me was pure malice . . . it was the only fly in the ointment . . . I couldn't help but love you, couldn't help but accept you, but I did have a feeling of guilt that I was probably taking my happiness at the expense of hers.'

He was staring at her. 'At the expense of hers? How could that be? She was nothing to me. And anyway, where on earth could you and Fenella have met? Or did she write to you? Did——'

'She came to see me in Auckland. She seemed to know more about Megan's affairs than I did—said you loved each other, only you were—were land-hungry. That owning Serenity meant everything to you. That despite all, she still loved you. She felt that if Megan had left half the estate to me, you might see marriage as the one way of getting control of the whole of it.

'Oh, it's all right, Gwillym . . . Don't look like that. I don't believe it, now. But it put me on my guard with you. Remember how prickly I was? How suspicious? But like you said the other night, we've been thrust into such intimacy, on a solitary sheep-run, that I recognised—finally—that you had too much integrity for that. Real values stand out in a setting like this. I began to put it down to jealousy . . . that I was coming up here. I thought there might have been some attraction to start with, but stronger on her side than yours. Only it receded in the last little while because we've drawn so close. You're the type of man I'd like to live with for the rest of my life.'

He kissed her. 'How glad I am that you worked it out for yourself! I don't blame you for believing it to start with, when I'd been so hateful to you. But with the putting on of that ring, on this our true betrothal night, there's no room for distrust any more, is there?'

'None,' she said firmly. Gwillyn looked down on her and said, 'I do believe you're not going to ask me another thing about it, so it *is* absolute trust.'

'Is there any more to ask? Well, it doesn't matter.'

'Oh, yes, it does. I'm amazed that she dared. Though I shouldn't be when I think of the trouble she caused up here. She must have thought she could poison you against me. And she'd nothing to lose, seeing she was fleeing the country. She was a girl with a chip on her shoulder. She'd been a teacher. Later we heard that she'd stirred up trouble at the school, somewhere in the North Island, with a married man. She wasn't likely to get another teaching position, so she took on this governessing stint.

'Perhaps she'd never succeeded in establishing a

permanent relationship with men and it soured her. If her nature had matched her looks it would have been all right. But she seemed to have a grudge against couples who were happy. She even tried to captivate Geoff. As if he'd ever look at anyone but Marie! He did the wisest thing, stopped her in her tracks. He laughed at her in front of his wife—said in a chuckling sort of way, "You're wasting your time if you're hoping to be one side of an eternal triangle, Fenella. Nobody makes my pulses go faster than Marie does." That turned the acid on. She marked this writer fellow for her next victim, and the poor man didn't realise the danger. She got him into a very iffy situation when his fiancée came up here for a weekend.

'I believe fireworks wasn't in it! The girl was so upset and so proud that unknown to anyone, she rang Queenstown, hired a helicopter, and took off while everyone else was down at the Bay having a picnic, save Reg who was writing. She simply left a note. That was when Geoff took a hand. But in between these two incidents she—gosh, this makes a chap feel stupid—she had a try for me. First time she came across on one of the tourist launches and pretended she thought there was one back, later in the day. So she had to stay the night. Twice she rode over—she's a good horsewoman. The second time I'd had it. The first time she said she'd not dreamed it was so far and she was bone-weary and saddle-sore, and was terrified darkness might overtake her on the road. I'll spare you a recital of the way she made up to me that night, it makes a fellow feel a fool.

'The second time——' he grinned reminiscently, and stopped, tantalisingly. Luenda prompted him. He continued, 'I'd been away from the home paddocks when she came. I saw her horse tied up. I'd been up the cattle-yards and my boots were indescribable. I took them off and came in. They were in the kitchen. Wilkie's face was a study. She was facing the door and I put a finger to my mouth.

'Fenella was spinning some subtle tale, that was hinting we were falling for each other but that it wasn't easy for a man to ask a girl to share his life when someone like Megan dominated him. Oh, it was a masterpiece! I've just given you the bare bones. Then Fenella stopped and waited for Wilkie to comment. She didn't. She kept quiet till Fenella got nervous, then said drily, "You've had an audience, but I doubt that there'll be any applause."

'She made a desperate bid to—oh, how can I put it?—throw herself on my chivalry. Her look beseeched me not to humiliate her in front of Wilkie, but I wasn't having any. I just said, "What arrant nonsense!" Isn't it odd? Afterwards I felt quite proud of myself for using that word. I had never used it in my life before! Then I said, "Look, I heard about the trouble you tried to make between Geoff and Marie and I know they're giving you just one more chance or they'll turn you off the station, so you'd better stop this sort of thing. Lucky for you Megan's in Arrowtown. Get on your horse and go! It's a long twilight and even if you arrive back without any skin on your backside, I couldn't care less." Very satisfying if horribly coarse!' He looked down on Luenda. 'I'm glad it didn't make you turn me down. It could have.' He kissed her.

'I came back from California and it became common knowledge that Megan had made provision for a girl and three children to come down here, and she assumed we'd be certain to make a match of it, I expect. She must have heard about halving the income and made up her mind you'd get half the estate if you stayed on. The business with the author happened before I got back, and she was working out her notice. On the way home she thought to make you feel very uneasy. Thank God you worked it out for yourself.'

'I started feeling suspicious when I found out Wilkie was Australian,' Luenda told him. 'Fenella had said Wilkie hated her because she was from there. That she hated all Australians.'

Gwillym chuckled. 'She'd never know Wilkie wasn't a Kiwi. Well, I'd like to go and tear her liver out myself, for what she might have done and for giving you some unhappy moments. However, it seems Reg Merivale did it for me. You've passed with flying colours, love. You asked me straight out. Oh, incidentally, George Stillman, the solicitor, and his wife, are coming over tonight. They're friends of the Campions, and George is tickled about this. Seems he knew a bit more about Megan's intentions with regard to you than either you did or I did. I rang him yesterday with our news, and he's tickled pink. I thought he'd never stop chuckling.

'Megan had written to him from California and told him quite frankly she'd made up her mind that you'd be the bride for me. What are you blushing for, love? That's fair enough, isn't it?'

Luenda said, mock ruefully, 'It makes me feel so manipulated.'

'That's so, but who cares? We made up our own minds. From what he says, she thought if you could take it for a year, it was bound to dawn on me that you were the one for Serenity. She didn't know how long she'd got, so thought if she said a year, that meant whenever she died, you'd have winter and spring here, the two worst seasons for weather. If you could take them, you'd take anything. As it happened, it didn't need that. But there was a proviso. If by any chance we got engaged before the year's end, her final dispositions were to be revealed then. George is bringing the papers across with him. We'll have a session with him some time tomorrow. Tonight is all skating and celebration!'

It was. Never had Luenda seen a more colourful spectacle. This beat an indoor skating rink hollow. Geoff had had the ice well tested, the courtyard where the barbecues were situated had a chestnut brazier there as well and the avenue of chestnuts that led off into the valley between the Twin Hills had yielded well. Oil flares were set around the rim, well back from the edge, and with the bright hoods and jackets of a community that had lived with winter sports all its life, the scene was reminiscent of a Dickens Christmas.

The twins had told Gwillym of Luenda's skating

outfits, and when she had refused to bring them along, saying she'd no desire to show off, he'd put the girls up to smuggling them out of Luenda's wardrobe into his suitcase. Meanly, he told the crowd what he'd done and they all clamoured for a display.

Marie, secretly, had steamed up the green velvet tunic and tiny widely flared skirt, fluffed up the white fur edging, pressed the scarlet briefs for underneath. Luenda came out of a dressing-room at the far end, pulled a face at Gwillym, and was away. Once she lost herself in all her professional standard twirls and loops and figures, she forgot her selfconsciousness and entered fully into the sheer joy of the movement.

As she sank into a curtsey at the end, she could have laughed her head off at the sheer pride on Gwillym's face. She contrasted it with the look on his face at the fashion parade!

Then she came to the edge, held out her hands to Claude and said with an audacious glance at Gwillym, 'My favourite partner ... Gwill, put on *The Blue Danube*, please?'

Laughing, he did just that. 'Nobody can waltz like older men,' she said, and they were away. Marie said dazedly to Gwillym, 'I don't believe it! I just don't believe it. That's old Dick Turpin!'

Then came the celebration supper. Luenda moved as in a dream. Could it be only three months ago she had lain and agonised over the situation she'd be left to cope with? Since that disastrous moment when Davy had brought in the man who'd looked his contempt of her at the parade? Since she had known the stomach-turning dread of having to live at close quarters with a man who regarded her as an interloper and opportunist? Now she was here ... loved and loving. All distrust was gone. Presently the whole household slept.

By mid-morning most of the crowd was skating again, but Gwillym and the solicitor said they had business to do. Gwill said to Luenda, 'We'll be in the office. We have a few preliminaries to get through before we call you in.'

She nodded. 'Claude is going to walk round the garden with me identifying these ground-creeping plants and the sub-alpine ones. I'm very impressed with the colour they manage to get in the garden here at this time of year. Our rockery is so drab. I thought if I could cover it with lichens and snowberries and all these tiny bright-leaved plants, it would make a patch of colour on the hillside and would be lovely. At present it's just lumps of grey rock.'

His eyes warmed. 'Have you been itching to get at it, my Luenda? Only you've never really counted it yours, till now. Go to it. Everything's yours now.'

She and Claude wandered happily. Seventy years and more among the mountains meant that he could recognise nearly every rock-plant and creeper of the South Island high-country. They were prolific, and Marie had told Luenda to break off pieces of all they fancied, so soon they had almost a basketful, and they restored the clumps to neatness as they went.

There was a choice rectangle of mosses in a corner where a wing jutted out, keeping it very moist. They stepped carefully over the separating rocks and crouched down, and Claude got busy with his sharp knife. Suddenly they heard the solicitor's voice. How odd . . . this was the opposite side of the house from the office.

It said, very clearly, 'Gwill, I don't really know if this is the right way to go about it. What does it matter now which one of you these belong to? You're going to be married. It could be transferred and she could know about it.'

Both Claude and Luenda paused in their gathering, crouching there under the window. They didn't look at each other.

Gwillym's voice was adamant. 'I want it this way. I must have it this way. I don't want to rouse her suspicions at all. She must never know there was any . . . er . . . skulduggery.'

Now Luenda and Claude stared at each other with a wild and reluctant surmise. Suspicion? Skulduggery?

Claude made an imperative gesture to her not to move.
She couldn't have, anyway. She'd just got to know what
it was about.

The solicitor's voice again. 'She's an intelligent girl.
What was she? Secretary to a big firm? Do you think
she wears blinkers?'

'I've told you my reasons and they stand. Just go
ahead, George. I know what I'm doing. I know Luenda.
She could back out if she knew the truth.' There was a
murmur too low to hear, then they heard him say, after
a few more unintelligible sentences from each, 'Then I'll
bring her in.'

Luenda clutched Claude, said in a low, intense
whisper, 'Get me out of here, Claude. Don't let him
find us yet. I—I—can't face him.'

Claude took one look at her stricken face and said,
'Over here. In the old cart-house.' They were over the
lake-stone cobbles of the yard in a trice, and into the
cobwebby shadows and refuge of the old building where
derelict drays and an old trap or two stood. There was a
wooden bench against one wall. Claude led Luenda
over there and sat her down.

She looked up at him piteously. 'What does it mean,
Claude? What does it mean? Is it as damning as I think
it is? What *can* it mean?'

He put an arm round her. 'Wheesht, now, lassie! I
can't bear to see you like this. It sounded odd—
inexplicable. But I've an advantage over you. I've
.known Gwill since he was in his teens, and he's not
capable of a dishonest act. Was it mebbe an
unfortunate way of putting it? . . . Skulduggery?'

She said forlornly, 'He said suspicion too. Doesn't it
add up to——?'

'Hush, let's think it out. It wasn't in context. We
don't know what went before it. I've known people do
good by stealth, and not want whoever they were
benefiting to know. They could say of that: "I don't
want them to have the slightest suspicion who's paying
for it." Now, couldn't they?'

The tumult in her heart stilled a little. Claude had

lived so long. He had a wisdom only experience could give. Then she burst out, 'But how can that be explained away? It must be about something coming to me from Megan.'

His voice was low, considering. 'It would seem so, indeed it almost certainly is, but we could be putting the wrong construction on it.'

She said bleakly, 'And only yesterday I was so happy! He even cleared up for me the doubts I had about Fenella Newbolt.'

A shrewd look crossed Claude's face. 'Ah, was she in it? And how?'

'Oh, she doesn't matter now. She came to see me in Auckland and said to be on my guard with Gwill, that he loved her but was letting her go because of Megan decreeing I should have this year on Serenity. She said he was mad for land, that he'd make up to me for sure, if he thought half the property was coming to me.'

Claude looked astounded. 'But the will's been read long since. They don't wait this long for probate. This can't be anything to do with the will. Who put that into your head?'

She faltered, her fierce indignation dying down. 'Why, I suppose Fenella did.'

Claude took her hands and said whimsically, 'Very, very like Letty. Always flying into a pucker about something. Don't you see, you're letting that poisonous Fenella still matter. You said Gwill had cleared it up about her. Luenda, don't let a big row brew up about this. It could harm your relationship at a very delicate stage. That lad's got to be asked what he meant—it's only fair. You're trying to be judge and jury rolled into one and you aren't allowing any defence. I admit it sounded bad, but it must be able to be explained. Gwillym is the man you've just promised to marry. You've got to trust him.'

Luenda gave a little moan, then brought up her left hand, gazed at the big emerald and the tiny diamonds and said, 'That's what he said when he put it on. He said: "I want there to be absolute trust between us, always." ' She stared at Claude. 'I just can't believe what I heard.'

He said gently, 'If you do trust him, you *won't* believe it. At least you won't believe the construction you and I put on it at first hearing. We got a shock. But you're going to face the two of them. And listen, girl, *you aren't going to look disbelieving*. You're going to make light of it. You're going to say something on these lines: "What on earth have you two been cooking up? Claude and I were digging mosses out under that window and we heard you. Come on now, tell us!" It's bound to bring results of some kind. But don't look scared when you ask, or accusing. I'm coming with you,' he added. 'They may tell me it's none of my business, but I'll stand my ground. If I'm to give you away, then I've got a father's rights. Now, pull yourself together and come on. I could hear him calling for you, but he seems to have gone round the other side of the house.'

They met Gwillym at the back door. Claude said, 'Sorry, we were sorting out this stuff in the cart-shed.'

Gwill looked very much at ease, with never a sign of guilt. He nodded. 'Better wash your hands, love, there are papers to sign.'

She said lightly, 'I didn't realise there'd be any of that. I thought I'd just hear what Megan had in mind.'

'There are some shares being handed over to you. There's a sort of receipt for you to sign. There's the tub.'

They washed their hands, dried them. Claude said, 'Luenda has asked me to be with her. I'm flattered—I feel I've got a family at last.'

Gwill did look surprised then, but Luenda was disarmed when he made no demur. 'Right, we're in that little book-room. One of Geoff's friends was in the office doing a lot of phoning.'

He led them in. Mr Stillman looked surprised too when he saw Claude, but Gwillym said easily, 'Luenda wanted Claude in on this. She looks on him as a stand-in papa.' Nevertheless, she noticed the solicitor, usually so urbane and unruffled, quickly shuffle some papers quite unnecessarily. She sent up a swift prayer, 'Oh,

God, please don't let anything be wrong. Don't let my trust be misplaced. Not *now*, God!'

The solicitor cleared his throat and said, producing a smile, 'Well, this is a pleasant occasion, one I've been looking forward to. It's a little out of the usual run, which even dry-as-dust-law men can enjoy. You know, of course, Luenda, that my late client, Megan Richards, knowing that her life-span was nearly over, and wishing to repay a favour your grandfather had done for someone she loved, and finding out your recent bereavement had left you in a very responsible position with regard to your half-sisters and brother, decided to give you a year on Mount Serenity Station.

'I might say, as I don't think you know this, that if she was given longer than the doctors thought, she intended to take you down with her. However, her time was shorter rather than longer.' He seemed more at ease now and smiled across the table at Luenda. 'She looked on Gwillym here as a son, and, having taken a great fancy to you, was desirous of the two of you meeting. She hoped you might take a fancy to each other.' He smiled again. 'As you have done. Not all matchmakers' plans proceed as ideally as this. You were given a year, and it's taken you three months.'

Luenda clasped her hands together in her lap to still their shaking. She felt the bulkiness of her ring and tried to remember she'd promised to trust Gwillym.

Mr Stillman continued, 'Her will had been made long ago. The half of the estate she still owned was to go to Gwillym.'

Luenda leaned forward. '*The half she still owned?* What do you mean? Didn't it all belong to her?'

Mr Stillman said quickly to Gwillym, 'Didn't you tell her?'

Gwillym said, and it sounded lame, 'I don't think it ever cropped up. It wasn't necessary. Half the income from the estate was to go to Luenda for this year. That seemed to take care of it for the time being. And of course now——'

'Yes, yes.' George Stillman was evidently trying to

stop Gwillym saying too much. 'Let's get on to this other thing. You did tell me you'd explained to her fairly recently that Megan had played the stock market disastrously some years ago. I thought you might have explained how we had to act then to save the estate. But yes, I can understand why you didn't.'

Luenda was trying to concentrate, a double line between her brows. 'But who owns the other half?' She mustn't let them sidetrack her. 'Who?'

The solicitor made up his mind. 'Mostly Gwillym's stepfather owns it. Gwill is now buying it off him, has been for some time. At first Gwill managed it for him when Guy retired. He'll be able to purchase it more quickly now that the other half is his, of course. He can raise money on that to buy the balance outright from his stepfather.'

Luenda's mind was sifting all this out. She had a quick look at Claude. He smiled at her reassuringly. So far, so good. Mr Stillman cleared his throat. He looked a little nervous again. Oh, stop being suspicious, Luenda, trust Gwillym. A light flashed in on her.

She leaned forward. 'When I was brought into this affair, there wasn't a new will made out, was there? I mean, this was just some sort of document Megan had made out in California when she knew her time was probably short?'

Both men looked wary. Mr Stillman said, 'Mrs Richards was ill and didn't fully realise the implications. She was away from her own men of business—myself, and her accountants, and she had a document drawn up to state what she wished. It would sound feasible, the whole thing. No mention was made of the fact that half the estate belonged to someone else.' Then he went on hurriedly, and she was sure it was in response to a look directed at him from Gwillym, 'But all that's beside the point. What we want to tell you this morning is that she knew she couldn't uproot you all without a substantial recompense, that even living free for a year was only a temporary aid, so she turned over some shares to you.

'This was in case nothing happened, in case you and

Gwillym were not attracted to each other. There's a letter here, most beautifully put, explaining this, that both of you must follow the dictates of your hearts in this matter, but if at the end of the year you felt you must return to Auckland, then these shares, sold, would give you the amount of capital needed to buy a modest house for the four of you. So we have the relevant papers here.

'I should also explain that in the event of your marrying Gwillym, this amount is to be yours in any case. Megan thought it was good for a woman not to be too dependent upon a husband, when, because of the isolation at Serenity, she had no chance of taking up her own work again. In your case, too, with three children dependent upon you, if you had enough to provide for them, it would never create any problem between you and Gwillym.'

He leaned back, and, she thought, looked relieved. She took a swift look at Gwill and recognised the same look there. He hurriedly summoned a smile for her. Mr Stillman said, 'Well, that's all. Is there anything you wanted to ask me before I get you to sign this receipt?'

Luenda glanced at Claude. There was a moment of complete rapport between them. He seemed to be feeling as she was . . . as if light was breaking in. She thought she knew what it was.

She leaned forward and said crisply, 'There is . . . oh, for sure there is. Gwill and his stepfather already own one half. Megan left her half to Gwill. Then where did my income from the estate come from?' There was a smiling light in her eyes.

Neither man answered her. They exchanged glances. They looked as if they hoped the other might speak first, be inspired.

She burst out laughing. 'Megan was too ill to realise that, wasn't she?'

Gwillym said hurriedly, 'Well, we followed the spirit of her wish for you. She wanted half the income from the estate to go to you, and even though I didn't know you as I know you now, I did want to carry out her last wishes.'

Luenda's eyes were very bright. She said quite calmly, 'Then this skulduggery and suspicion you were talking about when Claude and I were digging mosses out under that window there is more likely to benefit me than to cheat me, I take it?'

She could have laughed madly at the look on the two faces in front of her. Schoolboys caught out in a prank by their headmaster would register the same expression!

Gwillym gasped. 'You were there? What did you hear?' It wasn't guilt they were wearing, it was embarrassment.

The brown eyes danced. 'Well, you didn't want to arouse my suspicions. You didn't ever want me to know of your skulduggery. It was kind of Mr Stillman to say I was intelligent, that it wouldn't be easy to pull the wool over my eyes. Come clean ... for a horrible moment or two it gave Claude and myself an awful shock. We rushed away and hid in the cart-shed to get over it, and then ....' her voice wobbled, 'then Claude said something about trust.' She looked down on her ring, twisted it, and added, 'That made me remember I'd promised you so short a time ago that I'd always trust you. If there's skulduggery going on, I think it's to deceive me into thinking I bring the estate some money of my own. It's to give me some financial independence. I don't believe there *are* any shares. I think Megan was just giving me this respite of a year without any expense.'

Gwillym seemed to be seeking for words. Fortunately Mr Stillman found them first. 'This is coming out better than I hoped. I didn't care for what we were doing, even though Gwill was doing it with the most chivalrous motives. Gwill, I think more than ever now that you're a very lucky man ... in the bride you've picked. To trust you as she did after hearing that most ambiguous scrap of conversation.' He looked across at Luenda. 'There *were* shares. Megan *did* want you to have them only, they're worth practically nothing, like all her ventures. Gwill knew you had to see her letter, had to see the shares. He didn't want you disappointed. He was negotiating this even before you promised to marry him. He didn't know about the letter then—and what it might say—but he'd come to me and said that if ever you did decide to return to Auckland, he wanted the estate to recompense you in some way, if Megan had made no provision for you. When he rang me to tell me you were engaged, I opened the instructions, realised the shares were worthless, and Gwill instructed me to turn over to you some shares of his own. I might say he was going to sell them himself to help pay off his stepfather. He hoped that you'd never get to know they weren't Megan's.'

Claude so far forgot himself as to cheer. Luenda hardly heard him. She felt tears rushing to her eyes. Oh, how stupid to cry now ... she swung round, walked blindly to the French windows in the far wall, pushed them open and walked out on to the balcony that overlooked the lake.

She fumbled for a handkerchief. She heard the door bang as Claude and Mr Stillman left the room. She didn't know Gwillym was two steps behind her, didn't know till, as she reached the railings, two arms came round her, drawing her back against the hard, masculine strength of the man she loved.

She felt such shame, such humiliation ... all along she'd let the poison Fenella Newbolt had instilled work in her mind. Yet all that time, the whole estate had been, or would be, Gwillym's. Once his first fierce resentment of her had died down, he hadn't wanted her to know there was really no income for her to draw. She turned, tears still trembling on her lashes, 'Oh, Gwill, Gwill, the things I've said to you! And even then you wouldn't let me know. How did you keep silent?'

'Because I couldn't bear to have you go away from Mount Serenity. Couldn't bear it. And darling, do you know what pleases me most? The fact that you *did* finally trust me. That you had the courage to ask straight out what we were up to. Now we have no secrets from each other.' His green eyes, tender and laughing looked into hers. His mouth came down.

When, finally, they drew apart a little, they instinctively turned to look across the lake. Gwill's loved voice said, 'It's in full view, love. It's waiting to welcome us home in trust and love. Your Mount Serenity.'

Harlequin Plus

A WORD ABOUT THE AUTHOR

New Zealand-born Essie Summers comes from a long line of storytellers, and she herself began writing verse when she was only eight years old! By the age of ten she was composing short stories; at eighteen, submitting her writing for publication. It wasn't long after that she saw her poems, articles and short stories in print.

Although she says she loves dashing madly around and never walks if she can run, Essie often spends hours bent over a textbook searching for information that will affect perhaps only two or three paragraphs in her manuscript.

Her husband, Bill, a retired clergyman, is a "kindred spirit" who shares her delight in words and poetry. Today, she and Bill make their home in a picturesque town on New Zealand's North Island. They are the parents of two, and the proud grandparents of seven.

Essie Summers is a Harlequin author of long standing, having debuted in 1961. With more than forty books to her credit, she is also one of our most prolific writers. And, as readers around the world will confirm, she is one of the best loved.

Take these 4 best-selling novels FREE

Yes! Four sophisticated, contemporary love stories by four world-famous authors of romance FREE, as your introduction to the Harlequin Presents subscription plan. Thrill to **Anne Mather**'s passionate story BORN OUT OF LOVE, set in the Caribbean.... Travel to darkest Africa in **Violet Winspear**'s TIME OF THE TEMPTRESS.... Let **Charlotte Lamb** take you to the fascinating world of London's Fleet Street in MAN'S WORLD.... Discover beautiful Greece in **Sally Wentworth**'s moving romance SAY HELLO TO YESTERDAY.

Harlequin Presents...

The very finest in romance fiction

Join the millions of avid Harlequin readers all over the world who delight in the magic of a really exciting novel. EIGHT great NEW titles published EACH MONTH!
Each month you will get to know exciting, interesting, true-to-life people .... You'll be swept to distant lands you've dreamed of visiting .... Intrigue, adventure, romance, and the destiny of many lives will thrill you through each Harlequin Presents novel.

Get all the latest books before they're sold out!

As a Harlequin subscriber you actually receive your personal copies of the latest Presents novels immediately after they come off the press, so you're sure of getting all 8 each month.

Cancel your subscription whenever you wish!

You don't have to buy any minimum number of books. Whenever you decide to stop your subscription just let us know and we'll cancel all further shipments.